P9-DFY-354

"I'm scared of what the future holds."

Lauren reached for his hand and gave it a squeeze. That made it twice this morning that she'd touched him. Twice that such benign contact had zapped Gavin with all the force of a lightning bolt.

"If it were just me," she said, "I wouldn't worry so much. But with the baby?" She shook her head and her eyes turned bright.

"You're going to be fine. Both of you are going to be fine." He turned his hand over so that he could hold hers. She looked radiant. Sitting across from him, wearing a pair of shorts that showed off her trim legs, she looked lovely and…sexy.

Gavin swallowed. Was it okay to think of a pregnant woman as sexy?

Especially *this* pregnant woman?

Dear Reader,

I firmly believe that good things can come out of bad situations. Lauren discovers this when she decides to leave a loveless marriage to make a better life for herself and her unborn child.

I loved watching Lauren Seville develop her backbone page after page. Of course, Gavin O'Donnell recognizes her strength long before she does. In fact, it's one of the reasons he falls in love with her.

I hope you enjoy Lauren and Gavin's story. And may you, too, find a silver lining in all your dark clouds.

Best wishes,

Jackie Braun

JACKIE BRAUN
Expecting a Miracle

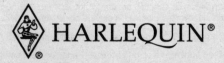

TORONTO • NEW YORK • LONDON
AMSTERDAM • PARIS • SYDNEY • HAMBURG
STOCKHOLM • ATHENS • TOKYO • MILAN • MADRID
PRAGUE • WARSAW • BUDAPEST • AUCKLAND

If you purchased this book without a cover you should be aware that this book is stolen property. It was reported as "unsold and destroyed" to the publisher, and neither the author nor the publisher has received any payment for this "stripped book."

ISBN-13: 978-0-373-17508-6
ISBN-10:   0-373-17508-6

EXPECTING A MIRACLE

First North American Publication 2008.

Copyright © 2008 by Jackie Braun Fridline.

All rights reserved. Except for use in any review, the reproduction or utilization of this work in whole or in part in any form by any electronic, mechanical or other means, now known or hereafter invented, including xerography, photocopying and recording, or in any information storage or retrieval system, is forbidden without the written permission of the publisher, Harlequin Enterprises Limited, 225 Duncan Mill Road, Don Mills, Ontario, Canada M3B 3K9.

This is a work of fiction. Names, characters, places and incidents are either the product of the author's imagination or are used fictitiously, and any resemblance to actual persons, living or dead, business establishments, events or locales is entirely coincidental.

This edition published by arrangement with Harlequin Books S.A.

® and TM are trademarks of the publisher. Trademarks indicated with ® are registered in the United States Patent and Trademark Office, the Canadian Trade Marks Office and in other countries.

www.eHarlequin.com

Printed in U.S.A.

Jackie Braun is a three-time RITA® Award finalist, a three-time National Readers' Choice Award finalist and a past winner of the Rising Star Award. She worked as a copy editor and editorial writer for a daily newspaper before quitting her day job in 2004 to write fiction full-time. She lives in Michigan with her family. She loves to hear from readers and can be reached through her Web site at www.jackiebraun.com.

"There's something inordinately sexy about a man who is as good with his hands as he is quick with his mind."
—Jackie Braun, *Expecting a Miracle*.

For Will, our unexpected miracle

CHAPTER ONE

LAUREN Seville pulled her car to the side of the road and stepped out. The summer day was gorgeous, the sky impossibly blue and bright with sunshine. Standing in front of a picturesque pasture in rural Connecticut, she breathed in the mingled scents of wildflowers and listened as the birds chirped and chattered overhead. Then she bent at the waist and retched into the weeds.

The day might be gorgeous, but her life was as unsettled as her stomach at the moment. She was pregnant.

Long ago—long before she'd met and married investment broker Holden Seville and had embarked on a career as the Wife of a Very Important Man—doctors had informed Lauren that she would never conceive. Now, four years into a marriage that had proved as sterile as she'd believed herself to be, she had.

She straightened and stroked her still-flat stomach through the lightweight fabric of her sundress. The news, received just two weeks earlier, still filled her with elation, awe and a sense of anticipation. She was nearly three months into what she considered a miracle.

Her husband did not share her joy about the baby. In fact, quite the opposite.

"I don't want children."

She could still hear the cold dismissal in his tone, but his words were hardly a news flash. He'd made that fact perfectly clear when he'd proposed marriage one year to the day after their first date. Children were disruptive, messy and, most of all, needy, he'd said. They were an improper fit for the career-and-cocktails lifestyle Holden enjoyed and planned to continue enjoying.

Lauren didn't share his view, but she hadn't argued it at the time. Why bother when the point was moot? Or it had been.

A fresh wave of nausea had her bending over a second time.

"Oh, God," she moaned afterward, staggering back a few steps to lean against the passenger side of her car.

How foolish she'd been to hope that her husband's rigid opinion would soften now that the deed was done. It still came as a painful shock to discover that he wanted it *undone*.

"End your pregnancy," he'd told her. *Your pregnancy.* As if Lauren was solely responsible for her state. As if he had no tie—by blood or otherwise—to the new life growing inside of her.

He'd finished his ultimatum with: "If you don't, I'll end our marriage."

So, a mere twenty-four hours after refusing, Lauren found herself standing alone on the side of a country road gazing at a pasture, feeling queasy, exhausted and longing for the comfort of the king-size bed in their Manhattan apartment. She would go back eventually. She'd left with nothing but her purse and painful disillusionment. But she wasn't going to return until she had formulated a plan. When she faced Holden again she would do so with dignity, with her hormone-fueled emotions under check. This time she would offer him a few terms and conditions of her own.

"Hey, are you all right?"

The deep voice startled Lauren. She swung around in time to see a man jogging toward her from the farmhouse just down the road. Good Lord. Had he seen…everything? Embarrassment turned her cheeks hot and she couldn't quite meet his gaze.

"I'm fine," Lauren called.

She pasted on a smile and headed around the car's hood, all the while hoping he wouldn't come any closer. But he continued down the road in a long-legged stride that brought them face-to-face before she could open the driver's-side door of her Mercedes and get inside.

Doing so now would be rude. Lauren was never rude. So she remained standing, lips crooked up in the same polite smile that had gotten her through many a tedious dinner party with her husband's work associates.

"Are you sure?" the man asked. "You still look a little pale. Maybe you should sit down."

Lauren pegged him to be in his midthirties and physically fit, if the nice sculpting of his tanned arms was any indication. He was average height with tousled, mocha-colored hair that the breeze teased into further disarray.

"I've been sitting. Well, driving." She waved a hand down the road in the direction she'd come. "I just stopped to…to…to stretch my legs."

"Right." Kind eyes studied her a moment. "Are you sure I can't get you a glass of water or something?"

"Oh, no. But thank you for offering."

It was a programmed response and so it slipped easily from her lips. She was used to lying about her feelings, subjugating her needs and putting a positive spin on everything. She'd done that growing up so as not to upset her workaholic parents' hectic timetables. She'd done that as a wife, putting Holden and his demanding career first. But she'd been driving for more than two hours with no particular destination in mind. She had no idea how long it would be before she reached the next town. At the moment the undeniable truth was that she had to use the bathroom and would trade her Prada pumps for a good swish of mouthwash.

So, before she could change her mind—again—she said primly, "Actually, I would appreciate the use of your…facilities."

"Facilities." She thought he might grin. But he didn't. He swept a hand in the direction of his house and said, "Sure. Right this way."

As they walked toward the farmhouse, he rested his

hand on the small of her back, almost as if he knew she wasn't quite steady on her feet. The gesture struck her as old-fashioned, gentlemanly almost. It seemed a little odd coming from a guy who was wearing a T-shirt whose logo was too faded to be readable and a pair of jeans stained on the thighs with various hues of paint.

She chided herself for judging him based on appearances alone. Lauren knew better than anyone that looks could be deceiving. She'd met enough designer-dressed phonies over the years. People who said all the appropriate things, supported all the right causes and knew which fork to use for their salads, but it was for show. She could spot them easily enough. It took a fake to know one.

Did anyone know the real Lauren Seville?

That thought had her remembering her manners. "I'm Lauren, by the way."

He smiled and a pair of dimples dented his stubble-covered cheeks. "Nice to meet you. My name's Gavin."

When they reached the house, he guided her up the steps to the porch and held open the front door for her. Curiosity had her glancing around when she entered his house. Beyond the foyer, the living room was bare of furniture unless one counted the sawhorse set up next to the fireplace.

"Are you working here?"

"Why do you ask?" But he laughed then. "Actually, I own the place. I'm in the middle of some pretty aggressive renovations."

"So I see."

He settled his hands on his hips and glanced around, looking satisfied. "The kitchen's coming along nicely and the bedroom on this floor is done. I'm just finishing up the crown molding in here. I'm debating whether I should stain it or paint it white. Same goes for the mantel I made. What do you think?"

That threw her. Gavin barely knew her and yet he was asking her opinion. "You want to know what I think?"

He shrugged. "Sure. Fresh eyes. Besides, you look like someone with good taste." His gaze skimmed down momentarily, his expression frank and appreciative, but hardly leering. It left her feeling ridiculously flattered.

And flustered. "You built the mantel too, hmm? You're very good with your hands."

"So I've been told."

Heat prickled Lauren's skin. Hormones, she decided. Fatigue.

Gavin cleared his throat. "The bathroom is down that hall, first door on the right."

"Thanks."

As she walked away, he called, "Ignore the mess. I'm in the middle of rehabbing that room, too."

He wasn't kidding about the mess. Shattered tiles from the walls lay in a heap in one corner and the light fixture was a single bare bulb that hung from a wire protruding from the ceiling.

Lauren stepped to the pedestal sink and turned on the faucet, half expecting to see the water come out brown. But it was clear and cool and it felt gloriously refreshing when she splashed some of it on her face. Though she wasn't one to snoop, desperation had her opening his medicine cabinet in search of something to help rid her mouth of its foul taste. She sighed with relief when she found a tube of toothpaste. She squeezed some onto her index finger and used it as a makeshift brush. When she joined Gavin on the porch a few minutes later she felt almost human again.

He was seated on the swing at the far end, a bottle of water in each hand and a cell phone tucked between his shoulder and ear. When she stepped outside, he ended his call, maneuvered the bottles so he could clip the phone back onto his belt and stood.

"Feeling better?" he asked as he handed Lauren one of the waters.

"Yes. Thank you."

"Good. Have a seat." He swept a hand in the direction of the swing he'd just left.

It looked comfortable despite its worn cushion. Comfortable and inviting, much like the man himself. More than anything she wanted to sit. Lauren shook her head. "I really should be on my way."

"Why? Are you late for something?" he asked.

"No. I just…I don't want to put you out. I'm sure you have better things to do."

"Nothing pressing. Well, the house. There's *always* something to do here." Gavin laughed. "But it'll keep." When she hesitated, he added. "Come on, Lauren. Join me. Consider it your good deed for the day. Once you go I'll have to get back to work. I'd appreciate the break."

"Well, in that case…" She smiled, and though it wasn't like her at all to spend time with a strange man in the middle of nowhere, she sat on the swing.

It creaked softly under her weight. She allowed it to sway gently. Wind chimes tinkled in the breeze. The sound was pleasing, peaceful. It took all of her willpower not to sigh and close her eyes.

Gavin settled a hip on the porch railing, angled in her direction. "So, where are you headed, anyway? If you don't mind me asking."

Lauren uncapped the water and took a sip. "I don't have a destination, actually. I'm just out driving."

"It's a nice day for that."

"Yes." Because he was studying her again, she glanced away. "It's lovely around here."

"You should have seen it in the spring when my orchard was in bloom."

"Orchard?"

"Three acres of apple trees," he said, pointing behind her.

She turned for a better look and could just make out some of the golf-ball-size green apples that had taken the blooms' places. Lauren had always lived in the city, first in Los Angeles and now in New York. She'd never called the countryside home. Even vacations had been spent in urban settings…Paris, London, Venice, Rome. But something about this place was vastly appealing. Peace, she thought again. Ten minutes on Gavin's front porch had had the same effect as an hour with her masseur.

"Have you lived here long?" she asked.

"No. I bought the place last year." He sipped his water before adding, "After my divorce."

"Sorry."

"No need to be. I'm not."

The reply was quick and matter-of-fact, but Lauren thought she detected bitterness. She wasn't sure what else to say so she settled on, "I see."

Gavin didn't seem to be expecting any sort of response. In fact, he changed the subject. "I like challenges, which is one of the reasons I bought this place. A few months after I began working on it, though, I got tired of commuting out from the city on the weekends. So, I decided to take an extended break from my job and I moved here."

She couldn't imagine Holden taking a break, extended or otherwise, from his job. Her husband ate, slept and breathed the stock exchange. Even their vacations rarely saw him out of touch with his office. It struck her then that even if he changed his mind about the baby she'd still be a single parent for all intents and purposes.

"You're frowning," Gavin said.

"Oh, sorry. I was just thinking about…" She shook her head. "Nothing." Then, because he was still watching her, she said, "So, you lived in New York?"

He sipped his water. "For the past dozen years."

She couldn't quite picture him there amid the sky-scrapers, bustling pedestrians and heavy traffic. Though she barely knew him at all, he looked like a man who enjoyed wide-open spaces and the quiet that went with them. Places such as this. And though Lauren had always been an urbanite, she could understand why.

"I live in New York," she said.

"You're not from there originally, though, are you?"

She blinked. "No. I'm a West Coast transplant. Los Angeles. How could you tell?"

Gavin studied her. He hadn't expected that answer. Something about Lauren seemed too soft, too uncertain for city life. Her looks certainly fit, though. He allowed his gaze to take another discreet tour from her perfectly coiffed hair to the heels of her fashionable pumps. He'd seen plenty of women who looked just like Lauren parading into Manhattan's private Colony Club or exiting their stretch limousines in front of the posh apartment buildings on Park Avenue. Still…

"You don't seem like a New Yorker," he said at last.

She surprised him by replying, "I was just thinking the same thing about you."

"I'm not a native, either," he admitted. "I was born and raised in a little town just outside Buffalo. Does it still show?"

"Not really."

But he thought she was being polite. He supposed given the way he was dressed and where they were sitting, her opinion made perfect sense. Perhaps she would see him in a different light if he was wearing one of the suits he'd picked up on his last trip to Milan and they'd bumped into one another at the Met. For one strange moment he almost wished that were the case. It had been a long time since he'd enjoyed the company of a woman.

"Do you like New York?" she was asking.

It seemed an odd question, but Gavin answered it anyway. "I loved it at first." He sipped his water and allowed his mind to reel backward. The place had been so exciting in the beginning and he'd just made a killing with his first big real estate deal. "What about you? Do you like it?"

She seemed to hesitate, but then she replied, "Yes. Of course. What's not to like? It has all of those wonderful restaurants, endless entertainment opportunities and incredible cultural attractions."

The response struck him as something she'd read in a tourism brochure rather than a heartfelt assessment. He eyed her curiously for a moment before nodding in agreement.

The conversation lapsed, but the interim was peaceful rather than strained. The swing creaked rhythmically, helping to fill the silence, and the wind chimes offered an abstract melody as the breeze ruffled the leaves of the big oak trees that shaded the better part of the front lawn.

He thought he heard Lauren sigh, which he took as a good sign. The woman was wound tight and clearly in need of relaxation. Gavin knew the feeling. Not all that long ago, he'd been that way, too.

"So, what made you decide to move here?" she asked after a while.

"I was looking for a slower pace." Which was true enough. He'd been working sixty, sometimes even seventy hours a week. He'd been on fire and then. "I burned out, big-time."

He couldn't believe he'd just shared that with someone—and a virtual stranger no less. Hell, he'd glossed over the truth with most of his family.

"This is definitely slower," she said. "It's a good place to think."

Gavin had done plenty of that. "Exactly."

"There's no traffic at all, no blaring horns, no choking exhaust. No…urgency." Her tone sounded wistful and sincere, as if something about her current situation made her appreciate the bucolic setting and the sluggishness that went with it almost as much as he did.

It prompted him to ask, "So, are you looking for a place in the country?"

"Me? No. I…" She shook her head, but then asked, "Why? Do you know of a place nearby?"

"This one will be on the market when I finally finish with it. But at the rate I'm going now, it probably won't be ready for a good year or so."

Her brows shot up in surprise. "You're going to sell it?"

"Sure. That's what I do for a living, more or less." The more being that usually the real estate he acquired was much larger and worth millions of dollars. The less being that he delegated the physical restoration and re-modeling work to others.

"So, this is just a job?" She sounded disappointed.

Gavin shrugged. "I guess you could say that."

Lauren flaked peeling paint off the armrest of the swing. She sounded wistful again when she said, "It seems more like a labor of love."

Labor of love? He'd considered the physical work to be therapeutic, wearing out his body so that his mind would shut down and take unpleasant memories with it. But now, as Gavin thought about the crown moldings, the mantel and the satisfaction he'd gleaned from crafting them, he decided that maybe Lauren was right. Still, he would be selling the house when he finished. He'd never planned to make this his perma-nent address. At some point he needed to return to New York and to Phoenix Brothers Development, the company he owned with his brother, Garrett. He couldn't hide in Connecticut forever, avoiding well-meaning friends and family, and foisting his respon-sibilities at Phoenix on others.

"So, you're not in the market for some real estate?" he asked.

Lauren frowned and her gaze slid away. "Actually, I am." She motioned toward the house. "But my needs are a little smaller than this house and a little more, well, immediate."

Smaller. The description was hardly what he'd

expected to hear. *More immediate.* An idea nudged him. An outrageous idea. Gavin ignored it.

"Are you…relocating?" He nearly said running. Why did that word seem a better fit?

"At least temporarily. Yes." Her head jerked in an emphatic nod as if she'd just reached a decision. "Do you know anything that might be available around here?"

"In Gabriel's Crossing, you mean?"

"Gabriel's Crossing." Her lips curved as she repeated the town's name, and Gavin got the feeling that before he'd said it Lauren hadn't actually known that's where she was.

That outrageous idea nudged him with a little more force. "Maybe."

"Is it nearby?" she asked.

"Very. There's a cottage about fifty yards behind the house. It's adjacent to the orchard, with great views out all of its windows. I lived in it myself before the rewiring of this place was complete."

"And it's for rent?"

It hadn't been. In fact, before this moment, Gavin had never entertained the idea of taking on a tenant. He certainly didn't need the income or, for that matter, the hassle. But he nodded. Then he felt compelled to point out, "It's not very big."

"It doesn't need to be big."

He glanced at Lauren's pricey clothes and Park Avenue appearance. The entire cottage could fit inside the master suite of his apartment back in New York.

He'd bet the same could be said for hers. And so he added, "There's not much closet space."

He was sure that bit of news would scuttle the deal. He almost hoped it would. He was being impulsive again. It was a trait that had all but doomed him in the past. But the lack of closets didn't appear to have any impact on Lauren's enthusiasm. Her expression remained a beguiling mix of hope and anticipation.

"Do you think I could see it?"

"You're interested?" Heaven help him, but Gavin knew he was, and it had nothing to do with a rental agreement. The woman was beautiful, enigmatic. He wouldn't mind unveiling some of her secrets.

For the first time since her arrival, his gaze detoured to her left hand. A set of rings encircled her third finger, and a whopper of a diamond was visible. *Married.* He nearly snorted out a laugh. *That's what I get for rushing ahead without thinking things through.*

Now if she took Gavin up on his hasty offer to rent the cottage, he would have a couple of lovebirds nesting within shouting distance of his house. Probably just as well, he decided, dismissing the spark of attraction. He wasn't in the market for a relationship. He hadn't been since his divorce. And although he missed certain aspects of female companionship, overall he didn't regret his decision one bit.

"I believe I am interested," Lauren said after a long pause. Her lips curved in a smile, and one of those aspects he had missed presented itself. "Do you think I could see it right now? I mean, if you can spare a little more of your time."

Gavin managed a grin as he straightened. "Sure. As I said, I've got nothing pressing at the moment."

Lauren stood in the middle of the cottage's main room. It was small—although the word *cozy* seemed a more apt description—and empty, except for some dusty storage boxes that Gavin assured her would be removed. She could picture an overstuffed chair and ottoman in front of the window that faced the orchard, and maybe a small writing desk in the vacant nook below the stairs. They'd already looked at the bedroom in the loft. It would be a tight fit, but it could accommodate a dresser and queen-size bed, as well as a changing table and crib.

"So, what do you think?" Gavin asked.

Lauren wasn't the spontaneous sort. Generally she thought things through carefully before making any decisions. Sometimes she even created lists, writing down the pros and cons of a situation and analyzing both columns in meticulous fashion before reaching a conclusion.

Not today.

Today was a day of firsts. Not only had she walked out on her husband, she was getting ready to lease a new home. A home for her and the baby.

"I'll take it." She swore she felt the leaden weight of recent events lift from her shoulders. "Maybe I should be spontaneous more often," she murmured.

"Excuse me?" Gavin said.

"Nothing. Just…thinking aloud. How much is the rent?"

Gavin scratched his chin thoughtfully before rattling off a sum that Lauren would have no problem affording. She'd hardly been a pauper coming into her marriage, and although she'd reluctantly quit her position six months before her wedding at Holden's request, she had a degree in advertising and prior work experience at one of the largest firms in Manhattan. She could always find a job if need be. For now, though, what she wanted was peace.

"Utilities are included," Gavin added as he waited for her answer.

She glanced around the room again, her gaze drawn to the windows and the outdoor beauty they framed. Another band of tension loosened. The peace she sought seemed included in the rent as well.

Turning to Gavin, she asked, "When can I move in?"

CHAPTER TWO

IT WAS late afternoon by the time Lauren returned to the city. She unlocked the door to the apartment slowly, dreading the confrontation to come. She should have realized whatever was left to say would be said in a civilized manner—civilized to the point of being impersonal. Just as her parents had never believed in arguing, neither did her husband.

She found Holden in his study, sitting in his favorite leather chair next to the gas fireplace, which was flickering cheerfully, its heat competing with the air-conditioning. Little matters like high utility bills and energy conservation were beneath him. He had enough money to be wasteful. It was one of the perks of being wealthy, he'd once told Lauren when she'd gently chastised him for leaving the water running in the bathroom.

She studied him now. He was an attractive man—polished, sophisticated. It occurred to her that she'd never seen him in blue jeans, either the designer variety or the kind faded from wear. Nor could she imagine him operating power tools or smelling of sawdust and sweat. He considered himself above physical labor of any sort. The only calluses on his hands were the result of his weekly squash game, and his muscular build came courtesy of the workouts he scheduled with a personal trainer in their home gym.

She cleared her throat to gain his attention, breaking what had been her parents' cardinal rule: always wait to be spoken to first. It struck her then how much it bothered her that she always felt the need to maintain her silence around her husband, too.

Holden glanced over the top of the *Wall Street Journal*.

"I already ate dinner, since I wasn't sure when you'd be back," he said. "I think Maria might have left something warming in the oven for you."

Lauren's stomach gave a queasy roll that had nothing to do with the mention of food. "I'm not hungry. Aren't you even curious where I went?"

"I imagine you went to Bergdorf's to work off your irritation," he said dryly. "How much did you spend?"

Was that actually what he thought? If so, then he really didn't know her at all. Even so, for the sake of the baby, she decided to try one last time to salvage their marriage. "I'm not irritated, Holden. I'm…horrified by the solution you suggested. We need to talk about this."

He folded the paper and set it aside. He'd never been a terribly demonstrative man, but at the moment his expression was so damningly remote that it made her shiver. It matched his tone when he replied, "I believe we already have."

"We didn't really discuss anything," Lauren argued. "You issued an ultimatum."

One of his eyebrows rose in challenge. "Yes, and you did the same."

She had. And she'd meant it. She could not, she would not, destroy the miracle growing inside her. Lauren sucked in a breath and straightened her spine. This made twice in one day she wasn't going to back down. "I'll be moving out. I found a place to live this afternoon. A cottage in the country."

Just thinking about a skyline of leafy trees rather than steel, stone and glass made it easier to breathe.

Holden blinked twice in rapid succession. It was the only sign that her words might have surprised him. Then he inquired with maddening detachment, "Will you require any help packing? Maria's gone for the day, but Niles is still here."

Lauren's composure slipped a notch. "That's it? I'm leaving, our marriage…our marriage is *ending*, and that's all you have to say?"

"If you're expecting me to fall on my knees and beg you to stay, you've been watching too much daytime television." He steepled his fingers then. "Of course, if you've changed your mind about the situation…"

"It's not a situation. It's a baby, Holden. We're having a baby."

The tips of his fingers turned white. "*You're* having

a baby. I do not want children. You understood that. You agreed to that when we got engaged," he reminded her.

"I didn't think it was possible. The doctors had told me—"

"You agreed."

"So that's it?" Lauren said softly.

"Hardly, but the lawyers will have to figure out the rest."

Had she really expected him to change his mind? She swallowed as another, more unnerving question niggled. Had she *wanted* him to?

Their relationship had never included fireworks. Even at the beginning, when everything was new and should have been exciting, true sparks had been in short supply. What had it been based on? she wondered now. Mutual interests? Mutual respect? Gratitude for the fact that Holden had accepted her, reproductive defects and all?

Lauren frowned. "Why did you marry me, Holden? Do you love me? Did you ever?"

He studied her a long moment before tipping his hands in her direction. "Why don't you ask yourself those same questions?"

As she folded clothes and placed them in her suitcases, Lauren did. She didn't like the answers she came up with.

CHAPTER THREE

GAVIN noticed two things about his tenant: she went to bed early and she kept to herself.

She had been living in the little cottage for nearly a month. Her lights were always out by eleven and he'd only bumped into her twice, not including the day she'd moved in with only one small van full of belongings and a check to cover the rent for an entire year. He'd requested only the first month's amount, but she'd insisted on paying the remainder up front and signing a lease, which he'd hastily drawn up on his computer.

In truth, he hadn't expected her to return at all. He'd figured her trip to the country had been a fluke and she would reconsider her decision to move here. For all he knew, she'd had a spat with her husband and once they'd kissed and made up she would regret her impulsiveness. He knew he was regretting his. But two days after shaking his hand while standing in the dusty cottage, she had come back with her spine straight, her gaze direct and determined.

She'd been all business that day, although he thought he'd detected exhaustion and maybe a little desperation behind her polite smile and firm handshake. Both had him wondering, but he'd managed to keep his curiosity in check. Not my business, he told himself.

On their two subsequent meetings, both of which had occurred at the mailbox out by the road, they'd exchanged greetings and the expected pleasantries, but they hadn't lingered as they had that first day on his porch. Nor had they spoken at any length.

Gavin found that he wanted to.

He was only human, and the enigmatic Lauren Seville inspired a lot of questions. What was the real story? The bits and pieces he knew certainly didn't add up.

For starters, women who looked and dressed like Lauren didn't rent tiny cottages in the country. Gabriel's Crossing was quaint and its four-star inn and three bed-and-breakfasts attracted their fair share of tourists year-round, but the town was hardly a mecca for New York's wealthy. It had shops and restaurants, but it lacked the upscale boutiques, trendy eateries, day spas and high-end salons that a woman from Manhattan's Upper East Side would not only expect but require.

And then there was the not-so-little matter of a wedding ring. The gold band and Rock of Gibraltar he'd noticed that first day had been on her finger when Lauren had handed Gavin her check for the rent.

Seeing it had prompted him to ask, "Will anyone be joining you in the cottage?"

She'd answered with a cryptic "Eventually."

Gavin assumed that someone would be her husband. But a month later the man had yet to put in an appearance. Spat, he wondered again? Or something bigger and more permanent?

"Not my business," he muttered again and got back to work.

He'd long finished with the crown molding in the living room and had trimmed out the tall windows that faced the road. Per Lauren's suggestion, he'd opted to stain both them and the mantel a rich mahogany. The room was coming along nicely, needing only a few patches in the plaster, fresh paint and a refinished floor to complete its transformation. Those could wait. He still had plenty of other projects to keep him busy. Indeed, every room in the house except the master suite had something that still required his attention. If this were a company site, a bevy of contractors would be working off a master list with the various jobs prioritized and deadlines for completion penciled in. But this project was personal and, well, cathartic, so Gavin worked at his own pace and on whatever suited his mood.

Today, it was laying the floor in the secondary downstairs bathroom. He'd chosen a tumbled travertine marble imported from Mexico. The sandy color complemented the richer-hued tiles he'd used on the walls. He planned to grout that later in the day—assuming he hadn't succumbed to heatstroke by then.

He reached for his water bottle and, after taking a

swig, used the hem of his T-shirt to mop the perspiration from his brow. It was not quite noon but it was already pushing eighty degrees in the shade. The house didn't have working air-conditioning yet. The guys from Howard's Heating and Cooling had assured him a crew would be out later in the week. In the meantime, Gavin had to make do with a box fan and the meager breeze that could be coaxed through the home's opened windows. He put in the earpieces of his MP3 player and got back to tile laying. He liked to listen to music while he worked. He preferred up-tempo rock, the heavier on the bass the better.

"Hello?" Lauren's voice echoed down the hall, somehow managing to be heard over the music blaring in his ears.

He was on his hands and knees, having just laid another square, when he heard her. He tugged out the earpieces and levered backward so he could peer out the door.

"In here," he called.

She'd pulled her hair back into a tidy ponytail and was dressed in a sleeveless white linen blouse that she'd left untucked over a pair of pink linen shorts. On another woman the outfit would not have been all that sexy, but on Lauren… Gavin swallowed, and the heat that blasted through his system had nothing to do with the temperature outside. He didn't remember her being quite so curvy.

Tenant, he reminded himself. *Married* tenant.

Even so his mouth went dry. The woman had a classy set of legs. He'd caught a glimpse of them that first day when she'd been wearing a sundress, but this outfit did a much better job of showcasing them. They were as long as a model's, and slim without being skinny. She had smooth knees, nicely turned calves and those ankles... He made a little humming noise as he reached for his water, not sure whether he wanted to drink the stuff or dump it over his head. God help him. He had a thing about ankles. He downed the last of the water and forced himself to look elsewhere.

"I can't believe you're working today," she said.

He shrugged. "What can I say? I'm a glutton for punishment." His gaze veered to her ankles again. "H-how are you holding up?"

The cottage had no air-conditioning, either, and unlike the house, where Gavin's bedroom was on the main floor, the only sleeping quarters there were on the upper level.

"I'm fine."

It wasn't the answer he expected. He figured she had come to complain. If he were renting the cottage, he would.

"I'm having the air-conditioning here fixed and I'll also have a unit installed in the cottage if you'd like."

"Yes. I'll gladly pay for it."

"No need. Unfortunately, it won't be today. It probably won't be till the end of the week," he said.

"That's okay. I'm fine," she said again.

"Do you always say that?"

Her brow wrinkled. "Sorry?"

"Fine. It seems to be your stock response."

"Oh, sorry."

"That's another one."

She frowned again, clearly not knowing what to say. For one bizarre moment, Gavin found himself wishing she'd lose her temper. He'd bet she'd look incredible angry.

"The tile looks terrific." More politeness, but he let it pass. He wasn't sure why he'd goaded her in the first place. Most landlords would kill for such an easygoing tenant.

"Thanks."

"You've obviously done this before."

"A time or two." Although not recently.

For the past decade, Gavin had been in charge of the big picture. He and his brother paid other people to see to the details. Theirs was a rags-to-riches success story, or so the *New York Times* claimed in a feature story they'd done on him and Garrett a couple years back.

The article had made it seem as if Gavin O'Donnell, businessman and self-made millionaire, had it all. But even prior to his divorce, he'd felt something was missing, that some vital part of himself had been lost. Little by little he was getting it back.

Lauren's voice pulled him out of his introspection. "You must enjoy working with your hands."

Indeed he did and not just on houses. Though Gavin fought the urge, his gaze trailed to her trim ankles again. He'd bet he could encircle one with his hand. He rubbed his damp palms on his jean-clad thighs. "Yeah. I haven't done it for a while, though. I forgot how, um, satisfying it can be."

"I thought you were a builder."

"I'm more of a give-the-orders, sign-the-check sort these days."

"Ah." She nodded. "The boss."

That was true enough, but he'd never been the type to go around proclaiming himself as such. He knew too many people who'd gotten wrapped up in their own importance. If a year in self-prescribed exile had taught him nothing else, Gavin had conclusive proof that the world didn't stop turning just because he'd opted out as a cog.

He decided to change the subject. "So, what can I help you with?"

"Oh. Sorry," she said. He grimaced. There was that word again. "I...I was wondering if it would be all right if I made some changes to the cottage."

"Changes?"

She cleared her throat. "Nothing major. I'd like to paint the walls in the bedroom."

The entire place was done in a serviceable white that was little more than a primer coat.

"Got a color in mind?" he asked.

"I'm leaning toward sage green or something along those lines," she said.

He nodded and scratched his chin, thinking of his already lengthy to-do list. "It might be a little while yet before I can get to that. The new cabinets for the kitchen are due to arrive next week. I talked a friend of mine into coming out from the city to help me install them." He grinned. "He said he'd work for a prime rib dinner and beer. Obviously, that's not union scale."

"I'm an even better deal. I'll do the work for free."

"You want to paint it yourself?" His tone held enough incredulity that she looked insulted.

"Do I look helpless?" Her brows arched and she crossed her arms.

So, the woman had a spine after all. Gavin nearly smiled. "Ever done any painting?"

"Some."

"Really?"

Her answer surprised him until she added, "Okay, no. Unless my toenails count."

Gavin's gaze dipped to her feet. The flat sandals she wore offered an unrestricted view of ten cotton-candy-pink-tipped digits. His ankle fetish now had stiff competition.

"You do good work."

Her shoulders lifted slightly. "It's all in the wrist."

"That so?"

"I could teach you," she offered. "I'm sure it's a skill that would come in handy on your next job site."

The beginnings of a grin lurked around the corners of her mouth. He liked seeing it. He liked knowing he'd helped put it there.

"I think I'll pass. Maybe I could just watch you paint

your own instead." The prospect was a bigger turn-on than Gavin wanted it to be.

Hell, *she* was a turn-on, standing in front of him in pastel linen and looking sexier than most women could manage in skimpy black lace.

They studied each other. For Gavin, awareness sizzled like the business end of a firecracker. The way Lauren fidgeted with her wedding ring had him half hoping, half worrying, that she felt it, too.

"I've been watching the home improvement channel," she told him after a moment. "I think I've picked up some decent pointers."

It took a second for Gavin to remember what they had been talking about. Paint. Painting. The cottage. "Oh. Good. Some of it's common sense. A lot of it is elbow grease. Technique only counts if you're being paid by the hour."

She smiled. "So, you'll let me do it?"

"Sure. I've got nothing against free labor. And if you mess it up—" he shrugged. "—it's just paint. Another coat or two and the place will look as good as new."

"I won't mess it up," she assured him.

"A bit of a perfectionist, are we?"

He didn't get the feeling she was teasing when she replied, "If you're going to do something, why not do it well?"

"Too bad everyone doesn't share your philosophy. So, are you free around three o' clock?" he asked.

"Sure," she said slowly.

"Good. We'll drive into town and swing by the hardware store. I need a few things, anyway, and while we're there you can pick out a paint color."

Lauren waited for Gavin under one of the big oaks, making use of the shade. She was just far enough along in her pregnancy that she could no longer button the waistband of most of her fitted clothes, but she hadn't suffered from nausea in more than a week.

She was sleeping a lot, but she wasn't sure if that was because of her pregnancy, the result of depression over her pending divorce or flat-out boredom. She wasn't good at being idle. Back in the city she'd found a way to fill up her life, which of course was far different than being fulfilled. But here she had no luncheons to attend, no committees to help chair, no dinner parties to plan, shop for and execute. After staring at the blank white walls of the cottage for nearly a month, desperation had forced her hand and she'd decided to approach Gavin with her proposal to paint.

Somewhere in the midst of talking wall colors, though, she'd begun noticing the day's growth of beard that shaded his angular jaw and a sweaty T-shirt that was pulled tight over some seriously toned shoulders. She fanned herself now, blaming her heated skin on the mercury. It wasn't the man. No, it couldn't be the man. She was pregnant, newly separated and several months from a divorce. Besides, she'd never been the sort to fantasize. Yet for a moment there…

She groped for a tidy explanation to this curious tangle of emotions. The best she could come up with was that she was confused, lonely and alone in a new town, staring down not just one major life change, but two. Gavin was nice, good-natured, easy-going and friendly. So, she'd flirted with him a little. No law against that. As for this unprecedented attraction? It was a figment of her imagination, a figment likely fueled by her hopped-up hormones.

When Gavin joined her, Lauren noticed that he'd shaved and had changed into a pair of cargo shorts and a fresh shirt. She thought she caught a whiff of soap, and his hair appeared to be damp from a shower. Because she wanted to keep looking at him, she turned her attention to the tree.

"This oak would be perfect for a swing," she commented.

Gavin regarded the thick branches for a moment. "Or a fat tire on a rope."

She shook her head. "No. A swing. Definitely a swing. And the seat should be painted red."

"Reliving your childhood?"

Hardly, she thought. "I lived in Los Angeles, remember? But I worked on an advertising campaign for an airline once. The commercial started off with a little boy swinging and making airplane noises."

"'Our pilots have always been eager to soar.'" Gavin grinned as he supplied the text. "I remember that slogan.

I didn't realize it was yours. For that matter, I didn't realize you'd worked…in advertising."

She got the feeling he hadn't thought she'd worked at all. "I don't at the moment. I left my job at Danielson & Marx four years ago."

"Danielson & Marx." He whistled low. "That's the big-time. Do you miss it?"

"Sometimes," she replied. She hadn't shared that truth with anyone, even her closest friend. When others asked the same question, she told them how content she was and how busy with committees and her crowded social calendar. It was easy to tell Gavin the truth, so she continued. "I especially miss the creative process. It's not easy to sell consumers on an idea or product with only a few words or images."

"I'm betting you were good at it."

She smiled, thinking of the four Addys she'd racked up during her relatively brief career, and admitted, "I had my moments."

He tucked his hands into the front pockets of his cargo shorts. "So, why did you quit?"

She bent down and plucked a blade of grass. As she tore it into small pieces, she said, "Well, I was getting married and…and…"

She released the last shred of grass and dusted her hands together without having completed the thought.

"Priorities changed," he allowed.

Lauren nodded, although she could now admit she

hadn't been the one to change them. She'd gone along to get along. She wasn't proud of that now.

"Maybe you'll get back into it at some point," he said. "With a big agency like that on your résumé not many places would turn you away."

"I could do that." Her portfolio was anything but mediocre. Lauren had been good at her job and had taken pride in her work.

"But?" He smiled, as if he knew she had something else on her mind.

Once again she found herself baring her soul. "What I'd really like to do is start my own agency, something that specializes in causes rather than goods and services."

"There's not a lot of money in that, but then you probably know that. It sounds like you've given the idea some thought."

"I have. But it needs more," she conceded. The idea had been back-burnered for a couple of years now, growing stale as Lauren had grown more complacent.

"This is a good place for thinking. And when you're ready to start out, I'm sure you have enough contacts you could probably pull that off," he replied.

She'd almost expected him to shoot down the idea. She had little doubt her parents and Holden would have, which perhaps explained why she'd never shared her dream with any of them.

"Thanks."

Gavin's brow crinkled. "For what?"

"For...for letting me paint the cottage."

CHAPTER FOUR

LAUREN had never been in a hardware store. Neither her father nor her husband was the sort to attempt any kind of home repair. The one in Gabriel's Crossing, however, reminded her of something from a movie, complete with a couple of older men sitting on a bench in the shade of the porch. If they'd been chewing tobacco or whittling sticks she wouldn't have been surprised. It turned out they were eating sunflower seeds and helping each other with a crossword puzzle. One of them apparently was the owner. He stood and shook Gavin's hand.

"Haven't seen you in a while. I was beginning to wonder if you'd finally given up on that old house and moved back to the city." His eyes crinkled with a grin after he said it.

"Never. I finish what I start, Pat. Besides, someone has to keep you in business."

"And don't think I don't appreciate it."

Gavin turned toward Lauren then. "Lauren, this is Pat Montgomery."

"Nice to meet you, Mr. Montgomery."

"No need to stand on formality here. It's just Pat." He divided a speculative look between them. "So, will you be visiting the area for long?"

"Actually, I'm not visiting. I've moved here…at least temporarily."

"Lauren's renting the cottage on my property," Gavin supplied.

"You don't say." The man's woolly eyebrows inched up, and his mouth twitched with a grin.

Lauren felt her cheeks grow warm. She had a good idea what he was thinking, and her pregnancy hadn't become obvious yet. Thankfully Gavin came to her rescue.

"Lauren was looking for a retreat from the city. Her husband will be joining her."

She'd left Gavin with that impression, she realized. Lying wasn't in her nature, nor was omitting the truth. Still, it seemed the wisest course of action at the moment. So, when Pat said, "I'm sure you and your husband will enjoy Gabriel's Crossing. It's a nice place to get away to," she replied, "Yes, I'm sure we'll enjoy it here."

"Paint's down that first aisle," Gavin said, pointing to the far side of the store. "I'll load up the two-by-fours while you make your selection."

"Okay."

About twenty minutes passed as she pored over paint chips. Lauren knew the exact moment Gavin came up behind her. She didn't hear his footsteps. Rather, she smelled soap. And though she wasn't quite sure how, she felt his presence. She was probably being silly, but something about him was welcoming, comforting. She wouldn't allow herself to consider the other descriptions that came to mind.

"I've narrowed it down to these two shades," she said before turning. "I've read that green is a relaxing color, perfect for promoting a peaceful night's sleep."

"One of the walls in my bedroom is red. Well, officially, crimson. I wonder what that's supposed to promote." Humor danced in his eyes. Humor and something else.

She swallowed the other completely inappropriate answers that came to mind and said, "Insomnia."

Gavin laughed and pushed a hand through his hair, leaving it in its usual disarray. "I don't know about that. I sleep like a baby."

The mention of the word *baby* helped banish the last of Lauren's wayward thoughts. "Sea foam." She held the paint chip out in front of her as if she'd just drawn a dagger. "What do you think?"

He gave the square of color his full attention. "It's tranquil."

"Perfect."

His fingers brushed hers as he took the paint chip. "I'll have Pat mix up a couple gallons and we can be on our way."

"Don't forget, I owe you an ice cream cone."

"I haven't forgotten."

As she watched him walk away, Lauren was left with

the impression that Gavin O'Donnell was the sort of man who never forgot anything.

"This is a popular spot today," Gavin said when they arrived at the ice cream shop.

The place was small with no inside seating. People were lined up six deep in front of the two order windows, and every available picnic table was filled. Children of varying sizes, apparently immune to the heat index, ran around on the lawn in an impromptu game of tag.

As they made their way to the window, a boy of about five hurtled headlong into Gavin.

"Whoa, partner," Gavin said, steadying him.

Another child took the opportunity to tag the boy's back. "You're it!" he hollered in glee.

As the pair dashed away, Gavin glanced down at his shirt and grimaced at the mark that had been left behind. Lauren knew exactly what Holden's reaction would have been upon seeing a chocolate smudge decorating the fabric of one of his shirts. For that matter, the child would not have gotten off without hearing a stern reprimand. But Gavin was merely shaking his head and chuckling wryly.

"I guess I should have left my old clothes on." He sent Lauren a wink as he grabbed napkins from a nearby tabletop dispenser and swiped at his ruined shirtfront. "This is what I get for trying to impress you."

He said it lightly, clearly joking. But Lauren was impressed, and it had nothing to do with what the man was wearing.

"You're very…" She said finally, "patient."

"It's just a shirt and he's just a kid." He shrugged, as if that explained it all. Lauren supposed that in a way it did. Gavin's easy-going reaction to the mishap summed up his personality.

"You'd make a good dad." She hadn't meant to say that. At least not out loud. And certainly not on a sigh.

Hearing the words didn't send Gavin into panic mode. He nodded. "I hope to one day."

"You want children?"

He looked slightly surprised by the question. "Not right now. But sure, eventually. Don't you?"

Lauren swallowed. The dashed dreams of the past and the miracle of the present clogged her throat. Before she could respond, a woman of about thirty rushed over to where they stood in line. She looked hot, harassed and, given the dark circles under her eyes, exhausted. And no wonder. She had a baby on one hip and a sticky-faced toddler in tow.

"Gosh. I'm really sorry about that." She motioned to the mark on Gavin's shirt. "That was my son, Thomas, who ran into you."

Gavin chuckled easily. "He left a lasting impression."

The woman shifted the baby to her other hip and began to rummage through a large purse that did double duty as a diaper bag if the package of wipes peeking out the top was any indication. After pulling out a piece of paper and a pen, she said, "Here, let me give you my address. You can send me a bill for your dry-cleaning."

"Oh, there's no need for that. Really," Gavin assured her. "It will come out in the wash."

"You're sure?"

"Positive." He reached over then and tickled one of the baby's many chins, delighting a giggle out of the drooling infant. "Looks like someone's cutting teeth."

The woman jiggled the baby. "Yes and he's making us all pay for it, aren't you, pumpkin?"

"Three children," Lauren marveled. "You certainly have your hands full."

The other woman snorted out a laugh. "And to think I used to want four. Of course, that was before the first one came along and a sound night's sleep became a distant memory. Thomas had colic." Just then her toddler started off in the direction of an overflowing garbage can. "I'd better go. Thanks for being so understanding about the shirt," she said to Gavin. Her gaze included them both when she added, "You know how kids are."

Lauren's polite smile slipped. No, she didn't know. In fact, she didn't have a clue. A tsunami-size wave of panic grew inside her. She would be finding out in the not-so-distant future, and she would be doing so as a single parent without so much as prior babysitting experience.

With her knees threatening to buckle, she whispered, "Oh, God."

"Lauren?" Gavin grabbed her elbow. "You okay?"

"S-sure. It's just that this line is so long," she hedged.

He winked. "The wait will be over before you know it."

That's what she was afraid of.

At the window she and Gavin made their ice cream selections—a plain vanilla soft-serve cone for her, a double scoop of chocolate fudge for him—and looked around for a place to sit. The tables remained filled, but an older couple was leaving a shady spot on the lawn. Gavin handed Lauren his ice cream cone, and before she could guess what he intended to do, he'd tugged the shirt over his head and spread it out on the grass under the tree.

"No sense both of us going home with stains," he said when she glanced at him in question.

"Thank you." She folded herself onto his shirt without protesting, mostly because it gave her something to do other than stare at his bare chest. The man had the body of a god. He was tanned enough to suggest he went shirtless when he worked outdoors. And he was toned, the hard contours of his chest softened only by a light dusting of dark hair.

"Better watch out," Gavin warned.

"Wh-why?"

"That's going to drip."

When she continued to stare blankly at him, he leaned over and licked her cone. Lauren sucked in a breath as she watched his tongue swirl around the ice cream.

He glanced up. "Sorry. I just…" He laughed then, a combination of embarrassment and amusement. "I can't believe I did that."

She couldn't, either. Nor could she believe what his benign gesture had done to her pulse. "Th-that's okay."

"Want some of mine?" He held out his cone. "Go ahead."

"No, thanks."

"Sure? It's chocolate fudge," he coaxed with a bob of his eyebrows.

"I like chocolate," she said softly. His eyes were the color of the semisweet, dark variety.

"Who doesn't?" Then he frowned. "So, if you like it, why didn't you order it?"

"I don't know. I guess vanilla seemed the safer choice given how quickly it's melting today."

"Do you always do what's safe, Lauren?"

She licked her ice cream before it could drip and then wrapped a napkin around the base of the cone. "I'm afraid so."

"Boring," he murmured.

"That's me. Borin' Lauren."

He laughed. "Was that your nickname when you were a kid?"

"Unfortunately."

"So, what did you do to earn it?"

"Nothing," she insisted, slightly offended.

He lapped up a mouthful of ice cream from his cone. "Come on, Borin' Lauren. Your secret's safe with me."

"If you really must know, I wouldn't sneak out after curfew with the other girls." When he frowned in confusion, she explained, "Summer camp."

"Ah. How old were you?"

"Twelve." Her parents had gone to Europe for a month, sprinkling their vacation with assorted business seminars and workshops. Lauren had started her period while they were gone. She wrinkled her nose at the memory. She'd felt so awkward and out of sorts that summer. She'd had no one to confide in other than a sympathetic camp counselor.

"I bet you secretly wanted to sneak out."

"Maybe, but I've always been a rule follower."

He studied her a moment. "Well, here's an opportunity to take a walk on the wild side." He snatched the cone out of her hand and replaced it with his. "Go on. Indulge."

"Oh, no, really—"

Before she could finish her protest, he added, "Better be quick about it or you'll be wearing it." Dark brows rose over a pair of amused eyes. "And I'm not going to come to your rescue this time."

She had little choice but to comply. She tried dainty licks at first, but as a river of brown began to ooze toward her hand, she gave up the pretense of manners and got down to serious business. She finished the first scoop before Gavin had put much of a dent into her vanilla. The second scoop was gone just as he was biting into the rim of the cone.

"You've got a healthy appetite when you let yourself go," he commented on a laugh.

Because she felt ridiculous and just plain happy, she

replied, "You'd better finish that one before I get done with yours or I'm taking it back."

"Keep eating like that, kiddo, and you won't be fitting into those shorts much longer," he warned lightheartedly.

She opened her mouth, ready to protest. In the end, though, she merely smiled.

Lauren was quiet on the ride back to the house. Gavin glanced over at his passenger a couple of times. She'd stretched out her long legs, crossing them at those trim ankles. Her hands were clasped over her middle. He thought she might drift off to sleep in the comfort of the truck's air-conditioned cab, but when they pulled into the driveway, her eyes were still open and that same secretive smile was playing around the corners of her mouth.

He'd had a nice time today. He'd forgotten what it was like to enjoy a carefree afternoon with a beautiful woman. Lauren had a surprising sense of humor lurking behind those finishing-school manners of hers. Maybe he'd invite her to dinner this evening. He had a couple of juicy steaks they could throw on his new state-of-the-art stainless-steel grill. His sister had sent the grill to him for his birthday last month, but he had yet to try it out. It wouldn't be like a date or anything. Nope. It would just be two people having dinner. Nothing wrong with two people sharing a meal, even if one of them was married, Gavin assured himself when his conscience kicked up.

He stopped the truck at the side of the house, trying

to work out the wording for the invitation as he shifted into Park and they got out.

"I was wondering if you would—"

A car pulled into the driveway and stopped behind Gavin's work truck. It was a Mercedes, a pricy silver model that appeared to be showroom new. The man unfolding himself from behind the wheel looked like something out of a showroom, too. He wore designer sunglasses, a linen shirt that somehow managed to still look crisp and tan trousers. The expression on his face was one of supreme irritation.

Gavin figured he was lost. He'd probably missed the turnoff to the interstate and was now irked beyond measure to find himself in this seemingly primitive little backwater without access to five-star accommodations.

"Need directions?"

The man peeled off the sunglasses. The eyes behind them were bright with annoyance. "Yes. Perhaps you can tell me where I can find my wife?"

CHAPTER FIVE

HER husband.

Gavin knew she had one of those, but he still felt as if he'd taken a surprise punch to the gut. He looked at Lauren, trying to decipher her expression. She didn't appear overly happy to see the man, even though they had spent the better part of a month apart. She wasn't falling into his arms. For that matter, she wasn't even smiling.

She looked surprised, apprehensive and nervous. Or was she feeling guilty? But then, maybe Gavin was transferring that last emotion onto her since it was what he was experiencing at the moment. He'd been about to ask her to dinner, although it wouldn't have been a date, he reminded his conscience for a second time.

"Holden." She'd gone sheet white. "I wasn't expecting you."

"Obviously," the man said drily, and his gaze veered to Gavin.

They eyed each other stoically, each man taking the other's measure as Lauren performed the introductions.

"This is my…" She hesitated just long enough to make them both uncomfortable. Holden's eyebrows notched up. "Landlord," she said at last. "Gavin O'Donnell. Gavin, this is Holden."

As the two men shook hands, Holden's gaze drifted to the side of the house where the paint was peeling and the trim was missing from around a couple of the windows.

"Nice place you have here." The words were as insincere as his smile was insolent.

Gavin gritted his teeth and replied, "It will be when it's finished. These things take time."

"And money," Holden said.

Gavin neither liked nor appreciated the implication in Holden's words, but he managed an easy shrug. "That's not an issue for me."

Lauren's husband said nothing, but his gaze took in Gavin's stained and wrinkled shirt before moving to the truck. It was a work vehicle and as such it would never win any prizes for its looks. Gavin knew what the man was thinking but he resisted the urge to get into a debate over who had the bigger bank account. His financial status was nobody's damned business but his own.

Lauren broke the strained silence. "The cottage I'm renting is back this way." She sent Gavin a smile. "Thank you again for today."

He gave a curt nod. "No problem. I'll bring the paint and supplies by later."

"Okay. That'll be fine."

As Gavin watched them walk away, he doubted Holden was going to roll up his sleeves and help her out.

Lauren was as surprised as Gavin that her husband had shown up. And not surprised in a good way. She'd had a nice day, one of the most pleasant and relaxing in memory. Part of her hadn't wanted it to end. She'd even been thinking about asking Gavin to join her for dinner, although what she would have cooked, she wasn't sure. Then Holden had arrived. One look at his mordant smile and mocking eyes and she'd felt all of the tension of the past couple months return.

She waited until they were inside the cottage to say, "You didn't mention you were coming."

"I prefer the element of surprise."

She ignored the underlying accusation. She wouldn't feel guilty. And she damn well wouldn't offer an explanation. If anyone was owed an explanation, it was she. So, turning to face him, Lauren demanded, "Why are you here?"

"I came to see if you've come to your senses."

She folded her arms over her chest. "About what?"

"Come on, Lauren. You've made your point."

"My *point*. Do you really think that's what my moving out was about?"

He sighed heavily and fiddled briefly with the earpieces on his sunglasses before using one to hang the pricey lenses from the open collar of his shirt.

"I want you to come home."

Home. Their lovely Park Avenue apartment no longer felt like home. In truth, it never had. No place she'd lived, either before or after her marriage, had seemed the ideal location to settle in for the long haul.

Until now.

She had too much else on her plate to ponder the implications of such a thought, so she pushed it away and dealt with the matter at hand.

"I'm still pregnant, Holden. And I haven't changed my mind about the baby."

She'd felt a strange flutter in her abdomen today on the drive back to the house. It might have been nothing. It might have been the result of too much ice cream, but she wanted to believe it was the baby and as such it had made the new life growing inside her all the more real and vital.

"I have," he said quietly.

Holden's reply shocked her, so much so that she wasn't sure she'd heard him right. "You've changed your mind about the baby?"

"Yes. I have." He reached out and stroked her arm. "I want you to come home."

The contact was as surprising as his words. Lauren tried to convince herself that she was happy about his change of heart. Their child could have two parents now, two parents who would love him or her and take an active role in his or her life. But something seemed off. Holden's next words were proof.

"I've done some thinking. Our lives really needn't be

disrupted too much. We can hire a live-in nanny to see to the child's needs."

"A live-in nanny?" Her lips twisted on the words.

"Don't say it like that. I had a nanny as a child. You had one yourself."

Yes, she had. Her parents had hired an assortment of caregivers and sitters until she'd finally been old enough to ship off to summer camps and boarding schools. Even when her parents had been home from work, her care and keeping had been relegated to others. Of course, as a single mom Lauren would have to make arrangements for the baby while she was at work, but Holden was talking about more than that.

Lauren placed a protective hand over her belly. "*I* want to see to *my* child's needs as much as possible."

"But how can you do that and find time to attend to the many other important things in your schedule?" He sounded truly baffled.

She was baffled, too. "What other important things are you talking about? I no longer have a career," she reminded him. Of course, lately she'd been going through her portfolio with an eye on future employment. She'd forgotten how good it felt to have the creative juices flowing.

"You know what I mean." He waved a hand in impatience. "You sit on committees, chair some of them. You run our household and see to our social engagements." *Our* meaning *his*. Everything in their marriage had revolved around him. "I have a dinner party coming up next week or have you forgotten?"

"Is that why you've come here today? Are you looking for a hostess?"

"Don't be ridiculous," he chided, but his gaze slid away, and Lauren figured she had her answer.

Before her pregnancy, she had been foolish enough to stay in a loveless marriage, but she wouldn't subject her baby to that stark, chilly atmosphere, especially when she had little reason to believe the climate would warm up. Sure, Holden was asking her to come home, and claimed he wanted their baby, but he didn't appear excited or overjoyed about impending parenthood. Rather, his expression was one of resignation. The image of Gavin tickling the baby's chin earlier in the day popped into Lauren's head. He'd shown more interest in and enthusiasm for a stranger's child than Holden was showing for his own. You'll make a good dad, she'd told Gavin. What sort of father was Holden going to be?

Sadly, she knew the answer.

Holden shoved his hands into his trouser pockets and stalked to the window. It was open, but the air was heavy and still. The lightweight, café-style curtains didn't so much as twitch. "God, it's sweltering in here," he snapped irritably. "Can't you put on the air-conditioning or something?"

Lauren sighed. This was Holden, never happy, never satisfied. Over the years she'd grown used to his constant complaints, but they grated on her nerves now. "There isn't any air-conditioning." She didn't bother to add that Gavin had promised to have a unit installed soon.

He turned to face her, shaking his head as he swept a hand to encompass the room. "Lauren, you don't belong here. God, this place is barely habitable."

She glanced around and saw character, charm and coziness, which was far more than could be said for their Manhattan apartment. Oh, it was tastefully decorated, but Holden had vetoed her every attempt to stamp the place with personality...her personality. She'd had no such restrictions in the cottage. Gavin was even allowing her to paint.

"I disagree. I like it here. I wake up in the morning to the sound of birds singing."

He rolled his eyes, unimpressed. "You can get that on a compact disc. The sound of babbling brooks and rustling leaves, too, if that's what you want."

Until just recently, so much in Lauren's life had been artificial and her relationship with her husband had been utterly superficial.

"I want the real thing." She wasn't talking about bird songs.

He seemed to realize that, too. His voice held a note of desperation when he said, "I'd like you to move back into the apartment. I think we can put this misunderstanding behind us."

I'd like...

I think...

She shook her head slowly. "No, Holden, we can't."

"What more do you want from me, Lauren?" he asked in exasperation.

He placed his hands on his hips. The pose was reminiscent of her lecturing father. It only served to reinforce her decision.

What do I want? She wanted what he wasn't capable of giving her or their child. She wanted what, through his actions and words, he'd made abundantly clear he would never be capable of giving: unconditional love.

"I've made a horrible mistake," she whispered at last.

Not surprisingly, he took her words to mean something else entirely. "I'm glad you finally see that. I'll call the movers and have you out of here by the end of the day."

Lauren closed her eyes and expelled a ragged breath. She felt exhausted and yet unburdened. "That's not the mistake I was talking about."

His eyes narrowed, his gaze hardened. "What are you saying, Lauren?"

"I'm saying I want a divorce."

Lauren followed the sound of hammering up the stairs to the farmhouse's second level. The blows were interspersed with a great deal of cursing. She found Gavin in one of the bedrooms, using a long-handled sledgehammer to break through the plaster on an interior wall. He was stripped to the waist and the tanned skin on his back glistened with perspiration that had soaked the waistband of his shorts.

"What are you doing?" she asked, as he raised the sledgehammer over his head and prepared to batter the wall again.

He whipped around, nearly dropping the heavy tool. He looked surprised to see her, and not necessarily in a good way. But then his face softened with an easy smile.

"Lauren. Hey. I didn't realize that you were standing there." He cleared his throat. "Everything... okay?"

"Fine. Everything's fine." Or it would be. She motioned toward the wall and the pile of rubble on the floor in front of it. "What are you doing? Besides making a mess?"

"This?" His shoulders lifted. "Just taking care of a little demo work."

"It seems awfully hot to be doing that today. Especially up here."

"I'm working off that ice cream." He winked.

Lauren's gaze lowered to a pair of incredibly ripped abs. No need for that, she thought. Every inch of the man's body was rock solid and, at the moment, glistening like something ethereal. She realized she was staring. Embarrassed, she forced her gaze to the wall. It sported a hole big enough for a man to fit through. "I'd say you worked off the ice cream and then some."

"It's good for frustrations, too," he admitted. "So, your husband getting settled in okay?"

"Actually, he's not staying."

"Oh." Gavin set the head of the sledgehammer on the floor and leaned on the long handle.

"Holden and I...we've been having some problems."

"Sorry to hear that."

"Thanks." She fiddled with the hem of her blouse. "He came here today to ask me to move back to the city."

"So, you've worked things out, then?"

"In a manner of speaking." Lauren smoothed down her hem and looked up. "I've asked him for a divorce."

Gavin's eyelids flickered in surprise, but other than that she couldn't gauge his reaction—nor was she sure why she wanted to try.

In fact, Gavin was floored. He didn't know what to say or why he felt so damned elated by her news. He kept his smile in check, though. Sympathy was called for at the moment. He reached out and gave her arm a squeeze. With as much sincerity as he could muster, he said, "God, Lauren, I'm sorry to hear that."

"Thanks."

"Are you okay?"

"I think so." She nodded vigorously. To convince him? To convince herself? Then, she added, "Ultimately this is for the best."

Gavin had felt that way too when he'd divorced, but it hadn't made things any easier at the time. He'd still felt mule kicked. So, he meant it when he asked, "Do you want to talk about it?"

Lauren studied him. "A man who wants to talk? But will you listen, too?"

He frowned. "Sorry?"

She closed her eyes, shook her head and sighed. "No, *I'm* sorry. That comment was insufferably rude."

And telling, Gavin thought. Very telling. It made one of her husband's deficiencies very clear. "It's okay. The offer still stands. So?"

But she was shaking her head. "I'm touched by your concern. Truly, I am. But as tempting as it is to unload, I don't think you need to hear all of the sad details."

He should be grateful. He should be relieved. Why was it he wanted to disagree?

Lauren went on. "Let's just say that Holden and I have a fundamental difference of opinion on a certain vital matter, and leave it at that."

That vague description certainly piqued his curiosity, but she looked so sad and fragile that Gavin could only respect her wishes. He nodded, and then found himself admitting, "My wife and I had one of those, too."

"Oh?"

"Yeah. She wanted to continue having an affair and I felt that wasn't in our marriage's best interests." God, why had he told her that? He snatched his wadded-up shirt off the floor and swiped it across his damp forehead.

"Ah."

He tucked a corner of the shirt into his back pocket and leaned against the handle of the sledgehammer again. "I demoed an entire cinderblock wall by myself after I found out she was sleeping with a good friend of mine. They're both exes now."

"That must have been awful for you."

Awful? He'd felt as if his world had been tipped upside down. But he merely shrugged. "The wall looked like hell, too. Only about a third of it was supposed to come down."

"Well, Holden's not cheating on me. He…he doesn't

want—" Her eyes grew wide before filling, and she covered her mouth in a futile attempt to muffle a sob.

"Oh, God! Don't do that," Gavin pleaded, doing a poor job of camouflaging his panic.

Lauren waved a hand. "Sorry." But the tears continued to course down her cheeks.

He thought he was beyond begging, but he did so now with unabashed fervor. "Please, Lauren. Please, don't cry."

"Okay." She nodded, but the tears didn't stop. "S-s-sorry," she sobbed.

Gavin felt helpless, too. What should he do? What should he say? Finally he told her the only thing he knew with utter certainty: "He's not worth it."

She stopped crying. Watery blue eyes studied him. He had her attention.

"He's not worth it," he said again, this time with more conviction.

Gavin pulled the shirt from his back pocket, but a glance at it told him it was far too dirty to be used to dry her tears, so he tossed it to the floor and stepped forward.

"You deserve better, Lauren. You deserve so much more." Cupping her face in his rough palms, he used the pads of his thumbs to gently brush aside the evidence of her heartache.

"Gavin."

"That's right." And it seemed so perfectly logical to open his arms. "Come here."

He might as well have said come home, because

that's how Lauren felt when she stepped forward, stepped into his embrace. His loose hold was foreign yet familiar. Home and heaven wrapped into one.

With one big hand he stroked her back, murmuring words she couldn't quite decipher. She didn't need to. At that moment she knew all she needed to know. She was safe. Someone cared.

As the seconds ticked by, however, feelings that were a bit more disconcerting began to stir. Gavin turned his head and Lauren felt his hot breath stir her hair. She became aware that she was pressed against his body, which was partially bared, sweaty and unyielding.

The hand stroking her back stilled, settling just above the curve of her bottom and her pulse picked up speed.

"Lauren?"

She swore he sounded just as surprised and confused as she was. She took a step away, fussing once again with the hem of her blouse to occupy her unsteady hands.

When she glanced up, Gavin was watching her. She saw his throat work, but it was still a moment before he was able to form words. That fact stroked her battered ego.

"So, you've asked for a divorce?"

She nodded. "It was never a very good marriage." The admission stung, but it seemed important to be truthful. "I want it to be over."

"I'm glad." He stepped forward and she thought he might reach for her again. Would he hold her? Would he kiss her? He did neither. Instead he stepped back. "For you, that is."

* * *

Later that evening, as the sun lowered in the sky and the temperature dipped to the low eighties, Lauren dialed her parents' number. She hadn't told them about the baby yet or about her troubles with her husband. Nor had she given them her new address and telephone number since if they needed to reach her they had her cell. But she'd merely been putting off the inevitable. It was time to address that.

Her mother answered on the third ring.

"Hi, Mom, it's Lauren." She was an only child and so giving her name was completely unnecessary. Lauren didn't like what it said about the relationship she had with her parents that she always felt the need to point out their kinship.

"Lauren, hi." Camille sounded harried and pressed for time. Sure enough, she said, "I'm just on my way out the door to yoga and your father is still at the office." The words, as well as her tone, were intended to discourage a long conversation. Nothing unusual there.

"Sorry." Lauren grimaced after offering the apology. Gavin was right. Lauren forever seemed to be issuing one. Clearing her throat, she said, "This is important, Mom."

There was a sigh and then silence. Finally, "What is it? Is Holden all right?"

"I'm sure he's fine."

"You've had a fight," Camille surmised.

"A fight? No." It had been far too civilized for that. "I thought you and Dad should know, I've asked for a divorce."

"Oh, Lauren." It wasn't sympathy in Camille's tone,

but a mixture of exasperation and disapproval. "Why would you go and do something like that? You were so lucky to find someone like him."

Lucky. For a time that had been how Lauren had viewed the situation, too. But even before Gavin had told her she deserved better, she'd reached that conclusion, as well. "Our marriage hasn't been good for a long time, but now…I'm pregnant, Mom. I'm going to have a baby."

She smiled as she said the last word.

"A baby? But how is that possible? You've always been told… The doctors have always said that you wouldn't be able to have children."

Camille's disbelief was not quite the reaction Lauren had hoped for. Her smile faltered as it became clear why it had taken her well over a month to call and deliver this astounding good news. How ironic, how *sad*, that while Lauren's gynecologist had hugged her after reporting the results of the pregnancy test and the nurse had actually grown misty-eyed, her own mother seemed too hung up on the mechanics of this miracle to simply rejoice in it.

"Is that all you have to say, Mom?"

"No. Of course not. It's just that you've taken me by surprise." Still, instead of asking when the baby was due or how Lauren was feeling, Camille's next question was, "What does Holden think about this?"

Lauren closed her eyes, breathed through her mouth and counted to ten in an effort to defuse her anger and mask her disappointment. She'd read about the technique in a self-help book and had used it often in recent years when interacting with her parents. Interestingly, her mother was a therapist.

"What does Holden think? I've asked for a divorce. That should tell you what he thinks."

"Lauren—"

She broke another of her parents' rules by interrupting. "He doesn't want this baby. He doesn't want his own child."

Lauren expected a little sympathy or she hoped for it at any rate. She should have known better. Camille said matter-of-factly, "Not everyone desires children."

Lauren pinched her eyes shut and called herself a fool. "Not everyone desires children," she repeated half under her breath. As if she didn't know that. She'd been raised by two such people before foolishly marrying one.

Camille was saying, "You need to understand what Holden is going through. This has to be a very trying time for him."

What Holden was going through? What about what *she* was going through? This was a trying time for Lauren, too. Her tone turned a little sharp when she said, "Sorry, Mom, but I ran out of understanding when he asked me to end my pregnancy."

"You're being unfair."

One...two...three... "The point is moot," she managed in a civil tone. "I moved out a month ago and today I officially asked Holden for a divorce."

"Raising a child on your own will be difficult," her mother warned. "Children need two parents."

"I agree wholeheartedly." She jerked her head down

in an emphatic nod, even though her mother couldn't see her. "But I'd rather my child had no father at all than one who doesn't want his life disrupted and is too busy with work and social engagements to make it to school plays or honor banquets."

She was talking about Holden, but apparently she'd nicked a nerve. In her best therapist's voice, Camille said, "You're projecting."

Lauren was undeterred. "I'm not a patient, Mom. I'm your daughter. And I'm not projecting. I'm stating a fact."

"Your father and I must have done something right while raising you. You turned out well," Camille countered. Her tone bordered on insulted.

Lauren would have preferred that her mother feel wounded instead. That emotion was more personal and far closer to what Lauren felt. She started to count to ten again, but she only made it past one before the pain she'd kept bottled up inside for nearly thirty years burst its cork.

"You didn't raise me at all. You and Dad hired a bunch of people to do it for you. You were too busy fixing other people's lives and Dad was too busy climbing the corporate ladder to take an interest in me. Me! Your only child." Her voice broke on a sob and a tear leaked down her cheek.

In contrast, Camille's tone was sharp with impatience. "We worked, Lauren Elizabeth. We had careers. We still have careers. Lots of parents do, you know. Your circumstances were hardly unique. Lots of parents work outside the home, and, I might add, you certainly benefited from our dual incomes. They afforded you a lot of opportunities and advantages. Other children would be grateful."

"You've had my gratitude." But Lauren hadn't wanted opportunities. She'd wanted their affection, their time, their attention and their unfettered love.

Camille made a little harrumphing noise. "You know, it's easy to judge others without walking in their shoes. You'll need to return to the workforce yourself if you divorce Holden."

"When."

"Excuse me?"

"When I divorce Holden." She heard her mother sigh and decided not to give Camille another opportunity to argue. "I'd better let you go, Mom. I've taken up enough of your time and I know you're eager to get to yoga. Be sure to pass the news on to Dad."

She hung up without waiting for her mother's response. Lauren was tired, but she'd never felt more determined.

As she rubbed the small mound of her belly she promised, "I'm going to be a good mom."

Gavin wasn't the sort to eavesdrop on a private telephone conversation, but the cottage windows were open. He was standing outside and when he heard Lauren's voice, laced with such pain and disappointment, he hadn't been able to walk away. Curiosity and something else had kept him rooted in place for the duration of her brief talk with her mother.

He could only hear Lauren, but he didn't need to listen to both sides of the conversation to know that whatever her mother was saying to her wasn't what Lauren had hoped to hear. And no wonder, given all of the drama going on in her life.

Not only had she left her husband and planned to divorce him, she was pregnant.

Pregnant.

And he'd held her in his arms earlier. Gavin scrubbed a hand over his face. Honesty demanded he admit he wanted to do much more. He wasn't sure how he felt about that. Hell, he wasn't sure about anything when it came to Lauren Seville. Sure she was beautiful, smart, too, and sexy in an understated way that had engaged his interest from the first. But the woman's personal life was a huge, untidy knot of complications.

The question was: did he want to help her untangle it?

There'd been a time when Gavin would have barreled ahead, consequences be damned. He would have gone with whatever his heart told him to do, even if his head wasn't in complete agreement.

Well, he'd paid for such impulsiveness. He'd paid dearly. So he pondered the question carefully as Lauren ended her phone call, and because he wasn't sure of the answer, he retreated from the cottage doorstep without ever knocking.

CHAPTER SIX

A COUPLE of weeks passed as Lauren mulled her future. She couldn't live in the cottage forever, even if her lease was paid up for a year. Also at some point she would need to get a job, which would require her to find child care. Perhaps she could hire on somewhere that had more flexible hours than her previous position or that allowed her to work from home part of the time.

Thinking about all of that was too dizzying, though, so she put together a list of the things she needed to do in the interim. Finding an obstetrician in Gabriel's Crossing and hiring a good divorce attorney vied for the top spots. Interestingly, telling Gavin about the baby ranked high, as well.

It wasn't that he needed to know as much as Lauren needed to tell him. Why, exactly, she wasn't sure. She could say nothing, of course, and eventually he'd figure it out on his own. But that didn't seem right. Especially when she recalled the way he'd held her the other day after she'd started to cry. She rubbed her arms now, remembering.

She swore something had passed between them. Something innocent and sweet and yet still promising enough to steal her breath. She couldn't help wishing she'd met Gavin under vastly different circumstances. Then she would have been free and perhaps brave enough to explore her feelings. But not now. Not with her life in such turmoil and hormones churning up her already agitated emotions.

So she would tell Gavin about the baby and hope for his friendship.

He was a good man—kind and patient and surely no more in search of romance at the moment than she was, given the way his own marriage had ended. Oh, he hid the scars well enough, but Lauren knew they were there. Friendship. Yes, that would be enough. More than enough. How she longed to have someone close by to share her excitement about the new life growing inside her. Recalling the way Gavin had reacted to the children at the ice cream shop, Lauren decided he would be happy for her.

She didn't have many close friends. Acquaintances she had by the dozen back in the city. True friends were in awfully short supply. That was her fault. She'd never been very good at making them. She tended to be too quiet, too reserved.

Wait to be spoken to, Lauren Elizabeth.

It had been her parents' cardinal rule, and she'd

followed it so religiously that it had become a hard habit to break.

She had managed to now and again, though. She still kept in touch with some of the women she'd worked with at Danielson & Marx. They lunched together on occasion. And then there was Lilly Hamlin, the one close friendship she'd maintained since her teens. She and Lilly had attended the same prep academy and remained in touch despite living on opposite sides of the country. But Lilly was busy chasing after twin toddlers these days and running an older son to this activity and that, so the two women rarely managed a lengthy phone conversation much less a visit.

Even so, Lilly was the first person Lauren had told about her pregnancy. Her friend had been absolutely delighted about the news and, later, when Lauren called to tell her she'd left Holden, Lilly had been supportive and understanding. Bless her, she'd also resisted the urge to say, "I told you so."

Her friend had never thought Holden good enough. Lilly and Gavin had something in common, Lauren mused.

At some point before the baby came, she hoped to fly to California for a visit. In the meantime, she would do her best to make friends here—starting with Gavin.

It was barely eight o'clock, but the heat in the cottage was already cloying, so she showered in cool water and then dressed in a blouse whose empire waist camouflaged her pouchy middle and allowed her to leave the button on her shorts undone. She pulled her damp hair back into a simple ponytail, put on a minimal amount of makeup and, satisfied that she looked presentable, left the cottage. She decided she would take a walk along the road first and then, when the hour was more reasonable, she would knock on Gavin's door, maybe invite him to the cottage for a cup of coffee or iced tea.

When she rounded the side of his house, however, she spied him outside standing atop a ladder under one of the oak trees. He was leaning across a thick branch securing the ropes that held a swing—a swing with a bright-red seat. It looked just like the one in the airline advertisement she'd coordinated. The one she'd told him about.

Lauren's grin unfurled slowly. "Good morning," she called.

He returned the greeting as he finished the job.

"You're up early," she commented.

"I could say the same."

"Yes, but I haven't been nearly as productive." She motioned with her hand. "Nice swing."

"Thanks."

"It's like the one in the commercial," she said as he began to descend the ladder. It wobbled a bit and so she rushed forward to hold it for him.

"I know. Our conversation the other day got me thinking."

"Oh?"

"My sister and her family are stopping in on Saturday for a couple hours on their way to visit her husband's folks in Hartford. I'm hoping a swing will keep the kids occupied and out of trouble during their visit."

Now on the ground, Gavin rested an elbow on one of the ladder's steps. The T-shirt he wore fit snugly across his chest. She told herself the only reason she noticed was because bits of tree bark dotted the fabric. Dragging her gaze back to his face, she asked, "How many do they have?"

"Grace and Mitch have three under the age of seven. All boys." Dimples dented in his shadowed cheeks as he grinned. "I think it's God's way of paying my sister back for the way she treated her two younger brothers while we were growing up."

"She was that bad?"

"Worse," he assured her. "*The* worst."

"And you and your brother were angels, I suppose?"

"Absolutely."

They both chuckled then.

"I wish I'd had siblings to terrorize me," Lauren mused. She recalled how lonely her childhood had been. How utterly solitary.

"Yeah. No kid should be an only child." Gavin's gaze lowered to her waist, almost as if he knew her secret. She sucked in a breath, reasoning that either way the opening was there to make her announcement and so she took it.

"I agree with you, but at the moment I'm grateful to be having one." She rested a hand on her abdomen.

A pair of dark brows drew together in concern.

"Everything okay? You're not…you're not having trouble with the baby?"

"No." She tilted her head to one side. "How long have you known?"

"Not long." He flushed as he explained, "I came by in the evening to see how you were doing the day Holden stopped in and I…I overheard you talking on the phone to your mother."

"Oh." It was her turn to be embarrassed.

"I didn't mean to eavesdrop. Honest. But the windows were open and it was hard not to hear what you were saying."

"It's okay," she said, even though she felt mortified.

He swallowed and his voice dropped to an intimate whisper. "Why didn't you say something before?"

Before what? she almost asked, but then realized he wasn't referring to a specific event. And why would he be? She lifted her shoulders in a shrug. "I don't know. It just never came up in conversation."

"I guess not. It's really none of my business anyway." He cleared his throat, and gone was that moment of vulnerability that had made her want to confide all sorts of things. "I mean, I'm just your landlord."

Just her landlord? Even though they hadn't known each other for very long, the description was all wrong. Lauren laid a hand on his arm. "You've quickly become a lot more than that to me, Gavin. I count you as my friend, too."

Even that description seemed lacking.

His head jerked down in a nod. "Same goes for me." Afterward, his mouth crooked up with an easygoing grin, although his eyes never lost their intensity. "You can never have too many friends."

But you could have too few, as Lauren knew only too well. Friendship required an effort. It required a person to reach out. Her hand was still on his forearm, but that wasn't enough. And so she said, "Have you had breakfast yet? I've got enough eggs to make an omelet and a really ripe cantaloupe that's just begging to be sliced and eaten."

"That's a tempting offer, but I should be getting to work."

"Oh." She dropped her hand and forced aside her disappointment. "Another time then."

"Yeah, another time." He hefted the ladder and folded it. With it braced against one shoulder he started toward the garage, but then he stopped and turned. "What kind of cheese do you have for that omelet?"

"Feta. It's one of the things I've been craving lately. I was thinking about throwing in some black olives. You know, kind of a Greek omelet."

His nose wrinkled. "Feta?"

"I also have cheddar."

"I think that goes better with the cantaloupe. Have you been craving that, too?" he asked.

It was her turn to wrinkle her nose. "No, but it's healthy."

He chuckled. "Well, I'm not much on cantaloupe

either, but an omelet—one made with *cheddar cheese*—now that sounds pretty tasty."

"Does that mean you've changed your mind?"

"It's a man's prerogative, too, you know."

She grinned. "I'm all for gender equality."

"Give me fifteen minutes to clean up and I'll be over." A smile tipped up the corners of his mouth and Lauren's pulse hitched. Friendship, she reminded her wayward heart. This invitation was all about friendship.

In record time Gavin had showered, shaved and changed into fresh clothes. When he arrived at the cottage his hair was damp and his cheeks still stung from the aftershave he'd slapped on. Lauren opened the door looking nervous and as lovely as ever.

That made *him* nervous.

They stared at each other for an awkward moment before she pointed to the package he held in one hand. "Is that for me?"

"Of course. My mother told me never to show up empty-handed. Besides, you can't have eggs without bacon. They go together."

She took the package and studied it a moment. "I can't say that a man has ever brought me a hostess gift like this before."

Her deadpan delivery surprised him, and so he tucked his tongue into his cheek and replied, "Well, flowers are so overdone."

They both chuckled and some of the awkwardness dissipated.

"Come in, please."

She stepped back to allow him entry. It was the first time he'd been inside since her arrival, and he noticed just how cozy and inviting she'd made the place without overdoing it on the decorating. Maybe he'd ask her advice when he was ready to put the farmhouse on the market. Staging was important and she had a good eye. The main living area was furnished in a neutral palette with accent pillows and wall art providing splashes of vivid color. In addition to the belongings he'd seen movers unload the day she'd arrived, more furniture had been delivered just the week before, including a maple kitchen set.

She pulled out one of the chairs. "Why don't you have a seat while I get started?"

"Need any help?" he asked.

"No, thanks. Can I get you something to drink? I can make coffee, although as warm as it is maybe you would prefer iced tea. Or juice. Orange juice. I have orange juice." The words came out in a mortifying rush.

Gavin lowered himself onto a seat. "Whatever you're having is fine. Relax, Lauren. I'm easy to please."

"Sorry."

She should have the word trademarked, he thought, but said nothing.

"I'm a little rusty at this," she went on.

"Rusty at what?" The words came out slowly.

She wrung her hands. "Friendship."

"Ah." In addition to feeling disappointed—an emotion he wasn't quite ready to explore—her explanation left him baffled. "Why do you say that?"

"I just am. I can throw a dinner party for thirty of Holden's work associates and their spouses, and make small talk with perfect strangers for hours on end, but you're…different."

"Different," he repeated, not at all sure he liked her use of that adjective to describe him.

"You matter to me," she added softly.

Gavin swallowed, not sure he liked those words, either.

"I don't have a lot of close friends," Lauren continued. "I'm not very good at making them."

"I find that hard to believe." Sure, Lauren was quiet and could be too self-contained at times, but he would hardly consider her antisocial.

"No, it's true." She sat in the chair next to his and with heartbreaking sincerity confided, "I'm scared, Gavin. I'm really scared."

"Of me?" The thought had his blood running cold.

"Of course not." She reached for his hand on the tabletop and gave it a squeeze. That made twice in one morning that she'd touched him. Twice that such benign contact had zapped him with all the force of a lightning bolt. "I'm scared of what the future holds. If it were just me, I wouldn't worry so much. But with the baby?" She shook her head and her eyes turned bright.

"You're going to be fine. *Both* of you are going to

be fine," he stressed, turning his hand over so that he could hold hers.

"This is all so new to me and I'm terrified I'm going to screw it up. I…I didn't think I'd ever have children," she admitted.

"Why?" He coughed then. "Sorry. That's an awfully personal question."

And Lauren struck him as a private person. Even so, she replied with utter candor, "That's what the doctors had always told me. I have a couple of medical issues that, according to them, should have made conception impossible."

He snorted out a laugh, eager to lighten the mood. "Just goes to show you what they know."

"Yes. I suppose so." But she still looked worried.

He squeezed her hand again. "It's called 'practicing medicine' for a reason."

At long last a smile teased her lips. Impending motherhood, rather than his stale quip, had put it there, he was sure. Lauren looked radiant. She looked lovely. Sitting next to him wearing a pair of shorts that showed off her trim legs, she looked…sexy. He swallowed and felt his palms grow damp. Was it okay to think of a pregnant woman as sexy? A still-*married* pregnant woman, his conscience reminded him.

His thoughts turned to her husband then. "So, what does Holden think about the baby?" Even as he asked the question, he figured he knew, based on the telephone conversation he'd overheard.

Her gaze drifted away. Some of her radiance dimmed. "He didn't want children when we married. Actually, it was a condition of his."

Gavin frowned in disbelief. "What do you mean? Can you put something like that in a prenup?"

"No, of course not. But he made his wishes on the matter very clear."

He'd only met Holden once and briefly, but Gavin had little difficulty seeing the guy as the sort who preferred pristine designer clothes and a foreign two-seater to sticky faces and the many demands of parenthood. But Lauren?

"Why did you agree?"

"I didn't exactly. As I said, I didn't think I could have children, so the fact that he didn't want them…" She left the sentence unfinished and shrugged.

"Made him perfect for you."

At his words Lauren glanced up sharply. Her mouth fell open and she drew back her hand.

"I'm sorry," he said. "That was a rude and presumptuous thing to say."

She shook her head but said nothing. A flush stained her cheeks, but he didn't think anger had put it there. Guilt? Regret? Surprise that he knew and in a way could understand?

Gavin went on. "So, this is the fundamental difference you mentioned the other day when you told me you were divorcing."

"Yes."

Lauren's hands were in her lap now and she was studying them. He did so, too, noting that she'd taken off her wedding ring and had replaced it with one that had an amethyst stone. She may have had a sentimental attachment to the new ring, but he got the feeling that Lauren was merely old-fashioned enough that she didn't want to walk around with a naked third finger on her left hand during pregnancy.

"Holden feels raising children is incompatible with the lifestyle he prefers," she said after a moment. The words came out in a pained whisper.

Gavin wanted to curse loud and long. He wanted to break something with his sledgehammer. Forget that, with his fist. Even more, he wanted to take Lauren in his arms as he had the other day. He wanted to hold her, console her…kiss her. He banished the thought and in a matter-of-fact voice said, "I'm sure he's right. Kids change everything, or so my sister has told me enough times. But marriage is about compromise."

Lauren glanced up. "Were you willing to compromise?"

The question took him by surprise. "When I was married, you mean?"

"Yes."

He shifted his feet under the table, disconcerted to find himself on the receiving end of a query that forced him to re-examine his own union. He'd much rather talk about hers.

Now he wondered, had he compromised enough?

Had he made the right choices, especially before Helena's affair when he'd worked such long hours? He'd thought so at the time, eager to get ahead, but maybe…

"I wanted our marriage to work. Hell, I didn't want to admit I'd made a mistake."

"No one likes to admit that," Lauren agreed.

She made it easy to confess, "I jumped into things too quickly. Maybe if I'd waited, hadn't rushed things, I would have figured out that Helena and I were just too damned different to make it for the long haul. The signs were there."

Blaring, neon signs that his brother, Garrett, had tried to point out. They'd wound up fighting bitterly over it, their relationship and business partnership suffering until Gavin had finally admitted the truth of Garrett's words.

"How long did you know each other before you got engaged?"

"A couple months." It had seemed like plenty of time back then, but he grimaced now and shook his head. "Then we eloped."

She made a humming noise. "That is quick."

"Impulsive is another word." He shook his head, regretting such spontaneity now whereas at the time he'd viewed the quickie ceremony in a tacky chapel in Vegas as exciting despite the doubts that had nipped him before their I Do's.

"You don't strike me as the impulsive sort," Lauren said. She cocked her head to one side, studied him. "You seem so laid back, so thoughtful about things, if the farmhouse renovations are any indication."

"Ah, but this is the new and improved me. I've learned the value of slowing down and taking the time to evaluate a situation before going off half-cocked." He shook his head and chuckled wryly. "Garrett—he's my brother—claims I'm no fun anymore."

"I don't know about that. I like the new and improved you. Very much." Was it his imagination, or did her cheeks grow pink?

"Thanks." It seemed only fair to admit, "I like the new and improved you, too."

Lauren blinked in surprise. "How do you know I've changed?"

"Because you're here," he said simply.

She nodded slowly and in a quiet voice admitted, "I've always done what was expected of me. I've listened and followed the rules and…" She lifted her shoulders as her words trailed away.

He'd suspected as much. "Not this time, though."

"No. Not this time." She glanced away and he saw her swallow. "I couldn't this time."

He wondered if Lauren realized she'd squared her shoulders as she said it. The woman was a paradox. She seemed fragile in many ways, but he glimpsed steel now and then, too. He liked it. "Good for you."

"Thanks, but I'm embarrassed that it took me this long. My marriage hasn't been good in…well, ever. But I stayed."

"Some lessons take longer to learn than others," he said.

"I guess so." Lauren stood and walked to the counter, where she'd laid out the ingredients for their omelet. As she broke eggs into a bowl, she asked in a wry voice, "So, having been there and done that, can you recommend a good divorce attorney back in Manhattan?"

"Depends on what you want," he said slowly.

"I just want it to be over so the baby and I can move on with our lives."

She poured some milk into the bowl and balanced it against her torso as she picked up the whisk. Steel, he thought again as she began mixing the ingredients with surprising force. Steel wrapped in velvet. Still, he felt the need to point out, "Be careful what you wish for. I just wanted to move on with my life, too, and it wound up costing me plenty in the settlement."

"I don't care. Holden can have it all. The apartment, its furnishings, our stock portfolio and other investments. I only want what I came into our marriage with. I have some savings set aside and I can earn a living."

"I don't doubt that you can, but your child is entitled to financial support from both parents. Even if you don't feel that way now, you may not want to tip your hand early in the negotiations," Gavin advised, feeling like the voice of experience.

She frowned. "That makes it sound like a business deal."

"Sadly, in a way that's what divorce is." He cleared his throat. "Have you thought about custody and visitation?"

She stopped whisking. "Holden doesn't want this

baby. He won't seek custody. I can't imagine he'll want visitation."

"That could change." When the bowl she'd been holding clattered to the countertop, splattering the front of her shirt with eggs, Gavin added, "Sorry, Lauren. I'm not trying to scare you, but people do and say all sorts of unexpected things when a marriage ends. Holden strikes me as the sort of man who cares a great deal about his public image."

She blotted at the mess on her blouse with a damp dishcloth. "He does. He sees it as an asset to his career."

"Then he's not going to want to be known as the sort of man who divorced his wife because she got pregnant with his child and then abandoned both of them physically and financially."

"I hadn't thought about it that way." Lauren gave up trying to clean her shirtfront. She gripped the countertop with both hands, as if seeking balance. No wonder. Her face had turned sheet white. "God, do you think he will actually petition for custody, either full or joint?"

"I don't know. I just think you need to be prepared."

"But he doesn't want the baby," she insisted. She wrapped a protective arm over her belly as her eyes turned bright. "I can't even bring myself to repeat what his first 'solution' to my pregnancy was."

Gavin was on his feet before her first tear fell. Where other women's tears had sent him fleeing, Lauren's drew him.

"Hey, hey. Don't do that. Don't cry. It's going to be

okay." He patted her shoulder awkwardly at first and then, remembering what it had felt like to hold her in his arms, he gave up trying to keep his distance. She needed him. He needed something, as well. And though he wasn't ready to explore the depth and breadth of his feelings, he could admit that when he held Lauren it felt right. He felt right and oddly complete.

"He doesn't want our baby," she said. This time the words were mumbled against Gavin's shoulder.

"It's okay," he promised. He'd make sure it was.

Lauren wasn't listening. "I won't let him have it. My child deserves better than to be raised by someone who's too busy to care. I grew up like that. I know what it's like." A sob shook her then and he was helpless to do anything but hold her. "I won't let that happen to my baby," she vowed.

"I'm sorry, Lauren. I'm so sorry." The words weren't intended just to comfort. He truly was sorry—sorry for the lonely child she'd been, sorry that the man she'd married had disappointed her so badly. Gavin hoped to God he was right when he said, "Holden probably won't want custody and, given what you say, it's a good bet he won't exercise any visitation rights."

She stayed in his arms for several more minutes, her hands resting against his chest.

"Thank you," she said as she pulled away.

"No need to thank me." He kept his tone light and though the truth had always been exactly the opposite he claimed, "I'm a sucker for a crying woman."

"I've been doing that a lot lately. Hormones." She sniffled, but thankfully sounded more like herself when she added, "Just for the record, I don't usually go around busting into tears and blubbering like a baby. I'm stronger than that."

"Yes, you are," Gavin agreed. He leaned over, unable to resist brushing her lips with a light kiss. Though his words were whispered, they were nonetheless sincere. "But you don't always have to be, you know. At least not with me."

CHAPTER SEVEN

AUGUST gave way to September, and Lauren had a grand view of the changes from the windows in her small cottage. The apples on the trees in the orchard began to ripen even as summer's lush greenery faded to a more subdued hue. Splashes of red and orange began appearing, hinting at the fall spectacle to come. In the evenings, the air carried a new crispness and the scent of wood smoke.

Lauren and Gavin had gotten into the habit of taking a walk as the sun was setting. Then they would retire to his front porch, sway on the swing, talk or sometimes just sit in companionable silence until the first stars appeared in the sky. She'd never seen so many stars, living in the city as she had all of her life. Out in the country, with no artificial light to detract from their brightness, they simply dazzled.

When the moon rose and the night grew too cool for comfort, Gavin walked Lauren to the cottage. Standing on her doorstep, he always kissed her good-night. It was a friendly peck, sometimes on the cheek, sometimes on the corner of her mouth. Holden had kissed her like that. Other people in her life had, as well. But this was different, remarkable in a way she couldn't define, though she'd lain awake at night trying to figure out how.

As the weeks passed, Lauren looked forward to that kiss, anticipated it even. And sometimes, when she finally nodded off to sleep, she dreamed about the man in a way that made it difficult to maintain eye contact when she saw him the next day.

So much was happening in Lauren's life. So much was changing, not the least of which was her body. She marveled at the way her abdomen had begun to bulge and her breasts had grown larger, fuller, heavier. Thankfully, they were no longer so unbearably tender, although they remained sensitive.

Lauren had found a new doctor in town, but meetings with her divorce attorney required her to make the trip into New York. Last night, as she and Gavin had swayed on the swing and he pointed out the constellations, he'd offered to drive in to the city with her.

"I have business in Midtown. I can drop you at your appointment and we can meet up afterward. We can have dinner before heading back," he'd suggested.

His idea was practical and she supposed environmentally friendly, as it conserved gasoline and put one less vehicle on Manhattan's congested streets. They were carpooling, nothing more. Yet the next morning it took Lauren nearly an hour to decide what to wear.

She knocked on the rear door to the farmhouse and

waited. Her smile faltered when Gavin answered. She'd gotten used to seeing him in faded jeans and worn T-shirts, his jaw shadowed, his hair a sexy, tousled mess. Today, however, he was dressed in dark trousers with a suit coat draped over one arm and the tie loosened at his collar. His usually messy hair was tamed and his jaw was freshly shaved.

"Good morning." Dimples flashed with his grin.

For the first time in her life, Lauren knew what it felt like to have her knees go weak.

"You look...wow," she managed to say at last.

He laughed self-consciously. "Thanks. You look pretty wow yourself, but then you always do. New shirt?"

"This? It's a maternity blouse," she admitted, tugging at the ballooning hem.

"It looks good on you."

"Thanks. I just threw on the first thing my hand touched when I reached into my closet," she lied. Then she bobbed her eyebrows. "Talk about looking nice."

He shrugged and repeated, "It was the first thing my hand touched when I reached into my closet."

"I didn't realize you shared one with Armani." Her gaze trailed over a tailored shirt that was tucked into a pair of charcoal-colored trousers. Neither had come off a department store rack, of that Lauren was sure. "You have excellent taste in clothes."

"I have an appreciation for craftsmanship and quality in all its many forms," he agreed.

Such craftsmanship and quality, as he put it, did not

come cheaply. Yet, Gavin didn't strike her as the sort of man who lived beyond his means. She tilted her head to one side. "Why do I get the feeling that you do more than restore old farmhouses out in the middle of nowhere?"

"Because I do. My brother and I own a business together. We buy and rehabilitate buildings in Manhattan."

"Like historic sites?" she asked.

"We've done some preservation work, yes," he said. "But generally speaking we convert older buildings to new uses. For instance, we might buy a warehouse and turn it into trendy loft apartments or remake it into office space. That's what today's meeting is about. We've found a buyer for a site we rehabbed in the Village."

What he was talking about took money. A good deal of money. Yet he'd never flaunted his wealth. She liked him all the more for it. "What's the name of your company?"

"Phoenix Brothers Development."

Her mouth dropped open at that. Though she'd already ascertained that Gavin was no pauper, she hadn't expected this reply. "Oh my God."

"Heard of us?" he inquired with a casual lift of his brows.

Indeed she had. His company's distinctive fiery logo had been plastered on some of the most gorgeously restored buildings in New York.

"Is it okay to be impressed? I wouldn't want to make you uncomfortable by gushing over your obvious foresight and talent."

He grinned. "Go ahead. Gush."

"You do incredible work, but you already know that."

"We try," he said modestly. "If you're going to do something, why not do it well? That can take time and investment, but it usually pays off."

Time…investment…pay off. They were talking about his work, about buildings, but his words could be applied to so much more.

So she asked, "What if it doesn't? I mean, aren't you ever afraid that you're going to pour your heart and soul into something and wind up with nothing to show for it afterward?"

"Sometimes."

He stepped onto the porch and pulled the door shut behind him. The move brought him close enough that she could smell the tangy scent of his aftershave and see the pulse beating at the base of his throat. "And yet you still…go for it?" she asked.

"Are we talking about your advertising firm?"

Her gaze strayed to the door beyond him and she concentrated on the chipped paint when she replied, "Among other things."

"Life is all about risks."

Lauren swallowed. "Then I guess I'd better start working up my nerve."

They faced each other, the only sound the far-off yapping of a neighbor's dog.

"We should…we should…" she managed at last. He was watching her mouth.

"Exactly."

Without waiting to find out what he was agreeing to, Lauren turned and started for his truck.

Gavin reached for her hand and stopped her. She turned, startled and oddly expectant, until he pointed to the garage.

"For this trip I think we'll take my car."

"Car?"

"The ride will be smoother."

Lauren doubted that.

The garage was nearly as old as the house and in a similar state of disrepair, but when he pushed up the battered wooden door, a shiny black Porsche was parked inside.

Lauren whistled. "Nice car."

"It gets me from Point A to Point B," he replied blandly, but then he grinned with obvious male pride. "And it gets me there fast."

The meeting with her lawyer didn't go exactly as Lauren had hoped. Her divorce was not going to be a simple or quick matter, if what she'd learned today was any indication.

She was drained emotionally and physically and felt dead on her feet as she waited for Gavin. Of course, her choice in shoes didn't help matters. The three-inch heels had seemed a perfectly logical choice to go with the A-line maternity skirt and lace-edged smock. But Lauren hadn't worn heels of any height in a couple of months. Her arches ached and so did her lower back. She shifted her weight and glanced up Eighth Avenue, hoping Gavin would be there soon. She was tired, frustrated and eager to sit down so she could discreetly kick off her shoes.

The Porsche pulled to the curb a moment later and Gavin hopped out and came around the hood to open the passenger-side door.

"Sorry I'm late. I spied something in a store window on the way here and had to stop for it."

"Don't worry about it." She glanced inside the car. A huge, pink-tutu-wearing teddy bear was strapped to the seat. Laughter tickled her throat as she said, "I gather this is the something that you had to stop for."

"Yeah. It caught my eye." He rubbed the back of his neck sheepishly. "So, what do you think?"

She thought it was perfect. She thought *he* was perfect. He'd given her baby its very first gift. Well, other than a cute yellow sleeper that Lilly had sent with a note of congratulations. But this was different. She glanced up at Gavin and her smile faltered.

"You don't like it," he said.

"It's not that." Lauren made her tone light. "I just didn't realize you were into girly stuffed animals."

"Very funny. It's for the baby."

"And it's adorable," she assured him. "Thank you."

"You're welcome." Gavin grinned as he unbuckled the seat belt and removed the stuffed animal. Standing on the curb with the teddy bear in his arms as traffic and pedestrians bustled by, he looked both ridiculous and sweet.

"What if the baby's a boy?" she asked.

His brows tugged together as if that possibility had never occurred to him. But then he shrugged.

"My gut's telling me it's a girl, but if I'm wrong the bear can lose the tutu and we'll outfit it in something manly."

She laughed. "It sounds like you've thought of everything."

"I try." He maneuvered the bear into the small space behind her seat and helped Lauren into the car. "So, any requests for dinner?"

"I don't care where we go or what's on the menu. Just make sure the place has long tablecloths."

"Excuse me?"

"I'm dying to take off my shoes."

And Lauren did. He saw her kick them off in the car on their way to Cartwright's, a steakhouse located on Broadway in Midtown.

In the late 1800s, the area where the restaurant was located had been home to some of the city's most fashionable retailers, which is why it had been called the Ladies' Mile. But times changed, many of the retailers moved elsewhere and for years some of the buildings sat empty and neglected. Then the area enjoyed a renaissance. A good number of the structures had been restored now, including the one that housed Cartwright's on its main level.

The building was one of the Phoenix Brothers' shining successes, so much so that afterward they'd kept it, moved their offices to the top three floors and rented out all of the others. Gavin had personally over-seen the detail work on the facade. He was particularly proud of the result and eager to gauge Lauren's reaction.

"I've never been here before," she said as they waited for the valet to reach them.

"The restaurant opened last summer. The upper floors of the building are office space. We're full up on tenants at the moment, but maybe something will be available when you're ready to start that advertising firm. I'll cut you a sweet deal." He winked, even as the breath backed up in his lungs.

Lauren's eyes rounded. "This is one of yours?"

He nodded.

"Oh, Gavin, it's gorgeous."

He accepted her compliment with a casual smile, but he was beaming with pride inside. Then he gave up acting nonchalant. "So you really like it?"

"I love it and I haven't even seen the inside yet. You must be really proud."

"I am." And touched by her enthusiasm. "You should have seen the before shot. It was in pretty rough shape inside and out when we bought it and began work."

"That's hard to believe now."

The valet, a young man who looked to be of all eighteen, arrived then. "Sweet ride," he said as Gavin got out and he got in.

Gavin leaned down and, with a wink in Lauren's di-rection, confided, "It's got more than four hundred and fifty ponies under the hood."

"Duuuude," was the valet's reverent reply.

Gavin knew just how the young man felt. "Take good care of her for me and there's an extra twenty in it for you."

"You got it."

While the valet climbed behind the wheel, Gavin came around to help Lauren out. She was trying to put her shoes back on and not having much success, partly because of the awkward angle. He crouched down in front of the open door.

"Here, let me give you a hand, Cinderella," he said on a chuckle.

He was merely being a gentleman, he told himself as he fished her shoes out from under the Porsche's low-slung dashboard. He would have performed the same service for his sister, for his mother. He would have done it for any woman, be she attractive or otherwise. It made no difference that Lauren was not related to him or that she had a face that would have made Helen of Troy seem plain.

He told himself that, but then Lauren shifted to swing her legs out of the vehicle. Her skirt hitched up, exposing her knees. He swallowed a groan and lowered his gaze in an effort to avoid temptation. That proved to be a huge mistake. There were her ankles, slim, inviting. He wanted to kiss them, then run his tongue over the silky skin. He sucked in a breath instead and let it hiss out slowly between his teeth.

"Gavin?" He glanced up. Lauren was watching him, and she wasn't the only one. Behind her, the valet was drumming his fingers on the leather-wrapped steering wheel, impatient to be off. "Are my feet swollen?" she asked.

Feet? He hadn't gotten that far down. He looked now. "Um, yeah. A little."

She nibbled her lip and peered at them. "I hope I can get them into my shoes."

"You're not the only one," he mumbled under his breath since the longer this went on the more likely he was to make a fool out of himself.

Cursing his nonsensical fetish, he got down to business, scooping up Lauren's right foot with one hand and the coordinating pump in the other. He mastered the task without incident, although when his fingers skimmed her ankle he slowed down and took a brief moment to enjoy the contact.

After straightening, he held out a hand to help her up.

"Thanks, Gavin."

"My pleasure," he said with a little too much feeling.

He coughed, regretting his inflection and mentally kicking himself for his word choice when a blush stained her cheeks. Had he embarrassed her? He was embarrassed. And growing steadily more frustrated. He wasn't sure how to proceed with Lauren. They were friends, of course, but he was also attracted to her. He'd been from the start. Sometimes he was all but certain the feeling was mutual.

Gavin hadn't dated since his divorce. Before Lauren, he hadn't been tempted to get back into the game, but he was tempted now. He'd been tempted for weeks. If she were any other woman, he would simply ask her out. If the first date went well, he'd consider a second. Maybe a third and so on. But there would be no strings. He might be ready to date, but he wasn't ready for strings.

Lauren wasn't any other woman, though. That was both a blessing and curse in this case. She was smart, sensitive, caring, lovely. In other words, special.

She also was off-limits. Way off-limits.

As they walked into the restaurant, he mentally listed all of the reasons he couldn't get romantically involved with her: She was his tenant. She was pregnant. She was vulnerable. And, legally at least, she was still another man's wife.

He waited for one of those reasons to douse his desire. None of them did, though, perhaps because when Gavin glanced over at Lauren she was watching him, clear blue eyes taking his measure. She didn't look embarrassed. She looked…turned on?

Maybe I'd better start working up my nerve. She'd mentioned that earlier and he'd convinced himself she'd been referring to starting a business. But what if…

He glanced away. He had to be wrong. Did pregnant women get turned on? Should they? Maybe it wasn't good for them in their condition. It certainly wasn't good for *his* condition at the moment. He couldn't think about this now. Not the time and certainly not the place. He pulled his suit coat closed and buttoned it.

"Food's excellent here," he said, talking louder than normal. "They have some of the best prime rib in the city."

"Great. I'm starving."

It was both comforting and disconcerting that Lauren seemed to be nearly shouting, too.

By the time the waitress brought their dinner salads, Gavin had wrestled all sexual interest back into submission. The four glasses of ice water he'd had to drink helped. As did the fact he and Lauren were talking about her divorce, resurrecting unpleasant memories from his own.

"I didn't realize the grounds for divorce in New York were so limited. It's going to take a lot longer than I'd hoped," she admitted on a sigh.

Dismissing his own disappointment, Gavin kept his tone light, "No 'irreconcilable differences' here, I'm afraid."

"I know. My attorney drew up the papers to document a formal separation, but Holden and I have to live apart for at least a year before a divorce can be granted."

"What does Holden say to that?" Gavin asked.

"He's no more eager than I am to see the matter drag out. I agreed to let him be the plaintiff." When Gavin grimaced, she shook her head. "It's a salve to his ego and it lets him save face with his colleagues to make it look like he's the one who wants out. I can only imagine what he's telling them about me and my reasons for leaving." But she shrugged. "Frankly, I don't care."

Gavin had a pretty good idea what the guy was saying about Lauren to anyone who would listen. He'd bet his half of Phoenix Brothers that all of it was as unflattering as it was untrue. "So, what does your lawyer think of that strategy?"

"He isn't very pleased with the idea. In fact, when I hired him to represent me, he tried to talk me out of it. But Holden and I had already reached a verbal agreement." She sipped her water. "Can I ask you something personal?"

"Sure."

"How long did your divorce take?"

Gavin shifted in his seat. "Longer than our courtship, but less time than it appears yours will. Of course, I had grounds."

"Adultery."

He nodded, remembering with painful clarity the moment when he'd walked into their apartment and found his wife and his best friend together. "It also helped to speed things up that I was willing to give Helena just about anything she wanted to make her go away."

"Do you regret that now?"

Gavin snorted out a laugh. "I regret a lot of things when it comes to Helena. I probably could have given her half of what I did in the settlement. I was the injured party, after all. But, I don't know, in the end I got the better deal."

She set down her fork and studied him. "Why do you say that?"

Why *did* he say that? Gavin had expressed a similar sentiment to other people on numerous occasions in the past year, but this time he actually meant it. Oh, the wound from his wife and his friend's betrayal continued to ache, but it wasn't because he still loved Helena. His pride had been nicked, his ego battered. Both were rebounding, right along with his heart. He was healing.

"Well?" she asked softly.

In place of his usual flippant response, he chose his words with care. "Because I'm free and I'm heart whole."

"Do you think you'll ever marry again?"

"I'm not ready now, but yeah," he said slowly. "When both the time and the woman are right, I'll marry." His gaze lowered to her stomach and he added, "I want a family. And you? Will you remarry?"

"I think so. But I won't make the mistake of settling again."

"You shouldn't," he agreed.

"Whoever I marry the next time will have to love my child as much as he loves me," she said.

Gavin's chest felt tight and his stomach took an odd little tumble. He blamed it on heartburn and the vinaigrette dressing on his salad. "That much is a given. I mean, the guy wouldn't be good enough for you if he didn't."

The waiter came by to refill their water glasses, and the strangely intimate moment ended. Afterward, he said, "My ex remarried."

"Was the groom your former friend?"

"Yep." His tone turned wry. "It goes without saying that I didn't attend their wedding even though the money she walked off with probably helped pay for their fancy nuptials on Maui."

"Maui," she repeated, raising her brows.

"Mmm-hmm. Anyway, last I heard, a couple months into wedded bliss they'd already tired of each other and had hired attorneys." He grinned. "Turns out they both were having affairs."

Lauren shook her head. "I guess it's true what they say. What goes around comes around."

"You've got to love karma."

What goes around, comes around.

Three weeks later, Lauren was mulling over that saying again and finding it hard to believe she'd ever done anything to Holden to deserve the bomb he'd dropped on her via the legal papers with which she had just been served.

He was citing new grounds for divorce: adultery. He even claimed to have proof—photographs that documented the affair. Pictures of what? Of whom?

Lauren leafed through the papers a second time, sure she'd missed something. None of this made sense. She hadn't cheated on Holden and he damned well knew that. Just as he knew the baby she was carrying was his, yet he'd left the unmistakable impression that he was not the father with his request for a paternity test.

He was being cruel by making such claims. Holden could be distant and distressingly cool on occasion, but cruel? She'd never seen this side of him, though now that she thought back on it, the wives of some of his colleagues had sometimes let slip that her husband could be ruthless in his quest to get ahead. She'd chalked it up to professional jealousy at the time. Now, however, Lauren supposed it just went to show how little she really knew or understood the man she'd married, and how little he knew or understood her if he thought she was going to take this claim lying down. The old Lauren might have. The new Lauren had grown a spine.

Through the window she spied Gavin walking toward the cottage. Leaves swirled at his feet and the breeze had his dark hair dancing. He was dressed for the crisp weather in a leather-trimmed barn jacket. The collar was turned up and his hands were stuffed into the pockets. She opened the door before he reached it.

His smile helped chase away some of the chill she was feeling.

"Someone's eager," he said.

Lauren had an appointment with her obstetrician in Gabriel's Crossing, and Gavin had volunteered to drive her to it since he had things to pick up at the hardware store in town. She easily could have driven herself. It was barely fifteen minutes away. But she liked Gavin's company, and she figured he must like hers, too, since he kept making such offers. Indeed, they spent as much time together as most married couples, probably more since his work didn't take him away from the farmhouse often.

Since their trip into Manhattan, their evening ritual had expanded to include dinner before their walk. They took turns with cooking, although as of last week they had begun preparing all their meals in Gavin's kitchen, which was now completely refurbished. Not only was his kitchen much larger than the one in the cottage, it had commercial-grade appliances that would have made a gourmet chef weep with envy. Lauren had had fun helping him pick those out, as well as the paint color for the walls and the tile work on the backsplash.

"Just let me get my coat," she said.

She attempted to scoot past him, but Gavin, ever perceptive, grabbed her hand and gently tugged her back. "Hey, everything okay?"

It was so tempting to tell him no and then lay out all of her troubles. He would listen, Lauren knew, just as he always listened. And he would offer insight and suggestions, just as he always offered insight and suggestions. If she cried—and, God, it was a good bet she would, given her wayward emotions—she knew she could count on him to dry her tears and then hold her in his arms and stroke her back with those big calloused hands.

So tempting…but she needed to start standing on her own two feet for her own sake, as well as for her baby's.

She worked up a smile and lied. "Fine. I'm just… tired. I didn't sleep well last night."

"Oh." He nodded. "Glad to hear it's only that. I saw the car arrive earlier when I was out in the orchard. I noticed the guy coming to your door. He looked like the official sort and it looked like he was serving you with some papers. I thought maybe it was something to do with your divorce."

Lauren sighed as her head dipped down. "You don't miss anything, do you?"

"Not where you're concerned." Gavin used his index finger to raise her chin, forcing her to look at him. "Want to tell me about it?"

His dark eyes were full of compassion and something else that always made it difficult for Lauren to breathe normally. And so she admitted on a sigh, "I do, which is exactly why I shouldn't."

Dimples flashed in his freshly shaved cheeks. "I'm afraid I'm not following your logic."

"I've been leaning on you too much lately, Gavin. Way too much. Even today, I'm letting you drive me to my doctor appointment again."

He frowned. "It's no big deal. Have I complained?"

"Of course not." And he wouldn't, she knew. "You're too much of a gentleman for that."

To her shock, he muttered a curse and stepped away. With his back to her, he gazed out the window. "I'm not always a gentleman where you're concerned, Lauren. Believe me."

"Gavin?" She rested her hand on his shoulder.

When he turned, the intensity in his dark gaze stole her breath. "I'm sorry."

"For what?"

He said nothing for a full minute. He just watched her as some private battle waged. Then he stepped forward, framed her face in his hands.

Just before his mouth covered hers he whispered, "For this."

CHAPTER EIGHT

HE INTENDED to stop. For that matter, he'd never intended to start. Off-limits, he reminded himself. Too many strings. The descriptions taunted him, because when Lauren's mouth opened in invitation beneath his, Gavin's intentions—right, wrong or otherwise—simply vanished. Need had no problem taking their place. Need so overwhelming, so intense and consuming, that it should have scared the hell out of him. It didn't. It excited him instead.

He stepped in closer and shifted the angle so that he could delve deeper. In response Lauren moaned softly and brought her arms up to his shoulders. Through the layers of his shirt and jacket, he swore he could feel her fingernails dig into his flesh. She leaned against him, full breasts and distended belly meeting the wall of his chest and torso. It was a different experience, he had to admit. Something—*someone*—was quite literally coming between them, and at the same time bringing them closer together. Gavin felt as protective of her unborn child as he did of Lauren.

And then there was this. He enjoyed spending his evenings with Lauren, but he didn't want to spend just his evenings with her and he certainly didn't want things to always end with a chaste peck at her door.

Warning bells sounded. He'd known Lauren mere months, not all that much longer than he'd known Helena when he'd foolishly proposed. Was he doing it again? Was he rushing ahead, letting emotions outpace reason?

He didn't want to think so. The problem was he couldn't think, at least not clearly, while he was kissing Lauren and holding her in his arms. He needed to stop, and then he needed to slow down until he was sure he wasn't repeating past mistakes.

He'd said he would marry again if both the timing and the woman were right. If Lauren was that woman, then once all other obstacles had been removed, their relationship would grow at a more sensible pace. In the meantime they would continue as friends. Just as Gavin reached that conclusion, Lauren pulled away.

"Oh God," she whispered and then covered her mouth with her hand.

The look of horror on her face registered with the same chilling effect as a bucket of ice water dumped over Gavin's head.

"Lauren, I'm sorry. I didn't mean to do that." He laughed gruffly then at his ludicrous explanation. The kiss could hardly be classified as an accident. So he added, "Well, I did *mean* to do that, but I shouldn't have."

Her response to his words shocked him. "I kissed you back."

Indeed she had. "It's okay."

"No."

"Please, don't be so upset about the kiss," he urged.

"I'm… I'm not upset about the kiss, Gavin."

But her face was still pale and her hands were trembling. "Okay. Then why do you still look so miserable?"

"I like you. *A lot.*"

"Same goes," he admitted. "*A lot.*"

Gavin thought she might smile, but she began shaking her head. "The timing—"

He nodded in understanding since she was essentially echoing his thoughts. "It absolutely stinks. I know that, Lauren. For me, too. But this doesn't have to progress anywhere." He inhaled deeply before going on. "In fact, it would be for the best if it didn't, at least for the time being. We've both got, um, issues to resolve and other things that need to take precedence." His gaze dropped meaningfully to her belly. "Neither one of us is really ready for a serious relationship. We can continue as friends."

That last word left a sour taste in his mouth, but, as solutions went, remaining platonic made the most sense for both of them. To his surprise, Lauren was shaking her head.

"I think I should move out," she announced.

Her words landed like a prizefighter's punch. "Whoa, whoa. Hold on a minute. That's not necessary.

Jeez, it was kiss." A kiss that still had his pulse jumping. "It's not like we slept together or anything."

"Holden's claiming we have."

Gavin staggered back a step, feeling pummeled again. "What?"

"He's alleging that I've been unfaithful during our marriage and citing adultery as the new grounds in our divorce. I think… I think you might be the other man he has in mind."

"That's ridiculous! We haven't done anything. Well, anything like *that*," he added.

"I don't know why he's doing this. I've never been unfaithful to him. He's even requesting a paternity test for our child," she said. "He knows perfectly well what the results will show."

"That son of a—" Gavin bit off the last part as well as the other coarser oaths that came to mind. "I know why he's doing this. He's using the tactic as leverage in the divorce, that's all, Lauren. He's threatening to make things ugly for you because he wants something in return."

She rubbed her arms as if chilled. "I guess so. But he's claiming to have pictures that document my supposed infidelity. I couldn't figure out what kind of pictures he could have, unless they were something he'd had doctored somehow, but now I'm thinking that they might be of you and me."

"Doing what?" Gavin asked, his voice rising along with his temper. "Taking a walk. Sitting on my front porch together talking. We haven't done anything."

"We've kissed before. Maybe not quite like we did just now, but in a photograph…"

He had the sinking feeling she was right. Gavin didn't care for the thought that some hired hack with a telephoto lens had been invading his privacy, any more than he liked the idea his very innocent relationship with Lauren could be turned into something sordid. He'd be having a word with Holden Seville. Right now, though, Lauren needed reassurance. Gavin hated seeing her so distraught. It couldn't be good for the baby, something her soon-to-be-ex clearly didn't care about.

"It's going to be all right." Gavin vowed that he would see to it. "He's just blowing smoke."

"I know. But I still think I should move out," she insisted. "It's not fair to you."

"Let me worry about what's fair."

"But—"

"If Holden wants to drag me into this, let him." Gavin would hire an attorney of his own if need be and sue the jerk for defamation. "I'm not guilty of anything. Nor are you."

He thought that would be the end of it, but Lauren said quietly, "That's not completely true. I am guilty of something. A moment ago, when you kissed me…" Her mouth worked soundlessly and she couldn't quite meet his gaze. Finally, she managed, "I never felt that way with Holden. *Never.*"

Gavin swallowed. How were they supposed to go

back to being just friends when she'd made an admission like that?

"This really complicates things," he said.

"I know."

Whether they intended to or not, whether they wanted to acknowledge it or not, their relationship was heading into uncharted territory.

Lauren was distracted that evening as they ate the roast and vegetables that had simmered in a Crock-Pot for a good portion of the day. More than half of the small serving she'd taken remained on her plate.

"Meat too well done?" he inquired as she pushed it around her plate.

"Wh-what?" She glanced first at Gavin and then down at her plate. "Oh, no. It's fine. Delicious. I just don't have much of an appetite tonight. Sorry."

"Did you call your attorney?" He'd suggested that on their way to her doctor appointment and Lauren had promised she would as soon as she got home.

But she was shaking her head. "No. I didn't get around to it. I'll do it tomorrow."

"You really need to. That's why you're paying the guy, to do the worrying for you." Maybe then she wouldn't be quite so pale.

"I know. Sorry."

"You don't need to apologize." It came out more sharply than he intended. Gavin moderated his tone and continued. "You're always saying you're sorry for things that don't require an apology, at least not from you."

"I'm…" She'd nearly said it again, but let out a sigh instead. "It's a habit, I guess."

"I know it is." He cleared his throat and decided to tell her something that had been on his mind for a while now. "I get the feeling a lot of people in your life have made you feel like you must be perfect and pleasant and agreeable at all times. And when you're not, you need to apologize. Well, for the record I don't expect you to be Mary Sunshine or the soul of accommodation every hour of every day. You're entitled to be distracted, tired, scared, confused, frustrated, irritated or just plain ticked off from time to time. Those are honest emotions that everyone experiences. You're entitled to experience them, too."

She didn't say anything for a long time. Then she admitted quietly, "My parents abhorred drama."

"Life is a drama." He shrugged. "Or it can be a comedy. When you're lucky, it's a little of both."

She smiled as he hoped she would, but then she went on and her words broke his heart. "I wasn't allowed to raise my voice. My parents considered yelling to be proof that I was out of control. My mother is a therapist."

He shook his head, irritated with them, sad for her. "At my house we had regular shoutfests. My folks didn't let them go on for very long, probably out of respect for the neighbors, but they let us blow off steam when it was necessary. Then they would step in, make us sit down and rationally explain what was wrong. We had to work together to figure out a solution." The memories had him smiling.

"Sounds very democratic," Lauren mused.

"Not exactly. Ultimately their word was final, but they took into account what we had to say."

"I wasn't allowed to speak out of turn or to interrupt adult conversations. I wasn't allowed to disagree with my parents either and, believe me, they never took into account what I had to say on a matter."

"So you learned to apologize."

Lauren nodded. "I did."

"What did they do to you when you rebelled or whatever? They didn't smack you around or anything?" His blood ran cold at the thought.

She laughed, but the sound held no humor. "No. They didn't like drama, remember."

"So what did they do?"

"They ignored me. That might not sound like punishment, but it was, especially since they weren't the most demonstrative or involved parents to begin with. Sometimes I almost wished they would hit me. It would have been less painful. We'd sit at the dinner table or our paths would cross in the living room and they wouldn't speak to me or even make eye contact. This went on for days. One time for nearly two weeks. I felt absolutely invisible."

Gavin left his chair and knelt down before hers, taking both of her hands in his. "You weren't invisible, Lauren. They were blind, and so is Holden. But I see you."

She kissed the knuckles he'd scraped leveling the bottom of a door just that morning. "Thank you."

Gavin pulled his hands away and cupped her cheeks. If nothing else, she needed to understand this. His voice was soft but insistent. "I don't want your thanks, Lauren. Do you hear me? I don't want gratitude from you. You don't need to apologize all the time, and you don't need to be so damned grateful just because I treat you the way you should be treated. The way you *deserve* to be treated."

He stroked her cheeks with the pads of his thumbs and because he was thinking about kissing her the way he had in the cottage, he let her go and rocked back on his heels.

He was rising to his feet when she let out a gasp. "Oh!"

Only the fact that she was smiling saved Gavin's heart from stopping. Even so, his stomach seemed to drop into his shoes. "What is it? Are you okay?"

"It's the baby. Here." She grabbed one of his hands and placed it on the left side of her belly. Almost immediately he felt something press against his palm. "Did you feel that?" she asked.

"Yeah." He kept his hand in place and felt it again. Grinning, he glanced up. Lauren was watching him. Her expression mirrored the wonder he felt. "What's she doing in there?" he asked.

"Playing soccer, I think." For the first time all day, she actually laughed. "*He* or she has been pretty active lately."

"You could find out, you know. You could just ask the doctor and end the speculation."

"And end the surprise, you mean," she chided.

"I'm not much on surprises these days."

Although he didn't say it, she knew Gavin's aversion to surprises had come courtesy of his divorce. The crumbling of her marriage had changed Lauren as well, but even more so, the credit went to the baby.

"Until the day I found out I was pregnant, I'd always hated surprises. But that was the best bit of unexpected news I've ever received. I've been a fan ever since."

"Well, boy or girl, either one is a gift."

Where Gavin had touched her with his heartfelt words about what she deserved, this left her staggered. With one simple sentence he'd turned her world on end and made her wish for the one thing that could never be: that he, rather than Holden, had fathered her baby.

"So how did the appointment go today?" he asked as he returned to his chair.

Lauren hadn't been terribly talkative on the drive back from town. In fact, and she wasn't proud of this, she'd actually feigned sleep to get out of having to answer questions such as this one. She couldn't feign sleep now.

"It went okay. Dr. Fairfield said the baby is developing right on schedule."

"So everything is fine?"

"Well, pretty much."

"Pretty much? What exactly does that mean?" he asked.

She fussed with her napkin before admitting, "My blood pressure was a little elevated today when the nurse checked it. It's probably just the stress."

"Is that the doctor's diagnosis or is it yours?" Gavin asked pointedly.

She sighed. "It's mine, but he agreed that stress could be the culprit."

"What does he suggest?"

"Nothing yet." Although she'd spent the afternoon on the Internet and knew that bed rest or an early C-section delivery could be in her future. She didn't mention those possibilities, though. "Just to be on the safe side he wants to see me again in a few days."

"I'll accompany you to that appointment," Gavin announced. Before she could argue, he added, "And I'm not just going to drop you off. I'm coming in. I want to know what the doctor thinks and to hear straight from him what you need to be doing."

Lauren was nervous. She wanted someone there. When she was being honest with herself she could admit she wanted that someone to be Gavin, but she said, "There's really no need for you—"

"Yes, there is. You're not going to do this alone. You don't need to." His voice dropped to just above a whisper. "I want to be there for you, Lauren. Let me be, okay?"

She could have argued, maybe she should have even. But she was so tired of being brave and pretending she wasn't scared. She was a strong woman. She knew that now. But she wanted the luxury of having someone to lean on from time to time.

"Okay," she agreed. "I'd say thank-you, but I've been warned not to."

Gavin smiled. "Who says you're slow?"

He'd expected more of an argument from her. The woman could be incredibly pigheaded at times. He supposed the fact that she'd given in so easily only showed how much she needed someone. Even so, when she left a little while later, she insisted she didn't want him to accompany her to her door.

"I'll be fine," she said when Gavin returned from the hall closet with both of their coats.

"Lauren—"

"No, really. Please. Let's just say good-night here," she pleaded. "Just in case."

Gavin sighed heavily and though he didn't like it, he agreed. He'd let her have her way on this.

He flipped on the back porch light and stood at the door, watching her walk the short distance to the cottage on the walkway he'd recently illuminated with landscaping lights. She moved quickly, despite her ungainly stride, and glanced left and right, no doubt wondering if someone was hiding in the orchard clicking off pictures.

He couldn't blame her. Gavin found himself wondering the same thing.

CHAPTER NINE

GAVIN phoned Holden at his office the next morning to set up a meeting. Lauren hadn't asked him to get involved. In fact, if she knew what he was up to she wouldn't be pleased. But he couldn't sit idly by and allow her and the baby to be subjected to this kind of stress.

"I can't imagine what we have to talk about," Holden said blandly at the beginning of their conversation. "Lauren behind on her rent?"

"I can think of a couple things. I'll come to your office," Gavin suggested. "Ten o'clock. Make sure you're free. I hate to be kept waiting."

"Fine, but I'll meet you someplace where you'll feel more comfortable," Holden replied with an exaggerated sigh.

"Gee, how accommodating of you," Gavin drawled. "There's a coffee shop near Rockefeller Center." He rattled off the address.

"Fine. But don't be late. I can't spare more than half an hour," Holden warned. "My time is at a premium."

"Mine, too."

"Yes, repairs to that house must keep you hopping," Holden said snidely.

"Those and a few other things," he agreed. He wasn't going to get into a mine-is-bigger-than-yours match with the man on the phone. "See you tomorrow."

Without Lauren riding in the passenger seat, Gavin switched the satellite radio from mellow jazz to a bass-thumping rock, turned up the volume to near deafening and shifted the Porsche into high gear, zipping along the highway at a rate of speed that would have earned him several points on his license had a police officer pulled him over. He arrived at the coffee shop in Midtown Manhattan a full twenty minutes before the agreed-upon time, figuring it would take him that long to find a parking spot. He got lucky, though, and secured one on the street in front of the café.

Despite Holden's claims of being busy, he was already there, seated at a table next to the window. When he spied Gavin stepping out of the Porsche, his eyebrows notched up in surprise, but by the time the two men were face-to-face inside the restaurant, the annoying smugness Gavin recalled from their first meeting had returned in spades.

"O'Donnell." Holden extended a hand whose palm was as smooth as a baby's bottom and with his chin motioned to the car parked outside. "You must have gotten one hell of a good trade on the truck."

He ignored the jab. "Hello, Seville."

The other man smiled. "And I didn't realize you had such good taste in clothes. That suit must have set you back a bundle." The smile turned sly. "But maybe you've met someone recently and you're thinking that money is no longer an issue for you."

The implication had Gavin seething, but he managed to say in a perfectly civilized tone, "We're not here to discuss either my clothes or my car."

"So I gather."

A waitress came by to refill Holden's coffee cup and take Gavin's order. He opted for nothing. He was in no mood for refreshments. When she was gone, Gavin got right down to business. "I'm not happy with your treatment of Lauren, and I want it to stop."

"I can't imagine how any of this is your concern...unless you've got a thing for my wife."

With Herculean effort Gavin ignored that taunt, too. "When she went to her obstetrician appointment yesterday, her blood pressure was elevated. Probably because of the stress you're putting her under with your ugly lies."

Holden didn't look overly concerned, even though he said, "I'm sorry to hear she's not feeling well."

"Yeah, I can see how sorry you are."

Holden shrugged. "It's not my fault."

Gavin wanted to shout, but he kept his voice low. "You're accusing her of having an affair. You're claiming that the baby she's carrying might not be yours. You don't think making groundless accusations like that causes a woman in her condition undue stress?"

"The accusations aren't groundless. I have some evidence that suggests the two of you are enjoying something more than a tenant-landlord relationship."

Holden's lips bowed with sharklike cunning, drawing Gavin's gaze to his teeth. Veneers. Had to be. No one had a smile that white and perfect without spending a serious amount of money and time at the dentist's office.

"We are enjoying more than a tenant-landlord relationship. Lauren and I are friends."

"*Just* friends?"

Gavin did his best not to remember the explosive kiss from the day before or the undercurrent of feelings that kept threatening to pull him in much deeper. "*Just* friends. As for your *evidence*, I don't think it will hold up in court since there's nothing going on between us."

"But you'd like there to be." The blinding smile made another appearance.

Gavin's temper flared again, this time accompanied by guilt. The two emotions made for an interesting combination and had his hands wanting to curl into fists. He laid his palms flat on his thighs instead and reminded himself that he was here on Lauren's behalf. Losing his cool wouldn't help matters. Indeed, he would be playing right into Holden's hands.

"What I'd like is for you to stop messing with her mind," he said evenly. "You know she hasn't been unfaithful. You know that baby is yours. I didn't even meet

Lauren until after she'd left you. She was already pregnant at that point."

Holden merely shrugged.

"In her condition she doesn't need any more stress," Gavin insisted a second time.

"I'm not trying to create stress for Lauren."

"It's just a side benefit, huh?"

"She made her own bed."

"Yes, and you were in it at the time," Gavin snapped. He experienced a surprising spurt of jealousy as he made the observation. He wasn't sure he'd felt this jealous when he'd learned Helena was having an affair. Betrayed. Yes, he'd felt that. But jealous?

Now was not the time to analyze his feelings.

"I have to look out for my own well-being," Holden was saying.

Gavin snorted. "And the baby? What about your child's well-being?"

"As you already know, I'm not convinced it's mine," Holden replied blandly.

"God, you're a piece of work." Gavin glared at the man. Didn't Holden know how lucky he'd been? Didn't he realize what he was letting slip away?

Apparently not, he decided, when Holden said, "I want this matter over and done with."

Gavin ached for Lauren. So many people in her life discounted her worth, marginalized her feelings. When she needed them, they let her down. Well, Gavin wasn't going to be one of them. Even if nothing beyond friendship ever developed between the two of them, he would show her the kind of loyalty, respect and trust she deserved. He would show her that she could count on at least one person to look out for her best interests.

He hardened his expression to match his resolve. "So, what's the bottom line?"

"I'm afraid I don't understand what you mean," Holden replied.

"Yes you do. What do you want from Lauren? You want something. That much is clear. That's why you're making this so difficult for her. So, what is it?"

"Are you her messenger boy now...among other things?"

"I'm her friend," Gavin stated succinctly for a second time. Not that long ago, he'd been in her shoes, disillusioned, bewildered and facing the end of his marriage. Oddly enough, his own heartache seemed a lifetime ago. The old bitterness was gone, the disillusionment erased. Had his self-prescribed sabbatical accomplished that or was it Lauren's doing?

"Very well." Holden folded his hands. "You want the bottom line, O'Donnell? Well, here it is. I've worked hard to get where I am. That's a concept you probably don't understand."

"I think I do," he said evenly.

"Then I'm sure you can appreciate that I don't intend to see my standard of living suffer because I have to support a second household."

"You're worried about alimony?" Gavin asked.

"Lauren doesn't want your money. She had a career once and she plans to again. She can support herself."

Holden rolled his eyes. "Not in the style to which she has grown accustomed." He glanced meaningfully at Gavin's suit. "Designer clothing don't come cheaply."

"That's not important to her."

"Wealth is important to everyone, especially those who've never had it." He sneered at Gavin. "And those who are about to lose it."

Gavin ignored the insult directed at him, but the one aimed at Lauren made him seethe. She was anything but superficial. He recalled the previous night, when the baby had moved. She'd been thrilled, awed and radiant with maternal love.

"How is it that you could have been married to her for four years and yet you don't know her at all?" Gavin asked.

"I know her well enough to know she's going to demand child support."

Gavin snorted and shook his head in dismay. "She shouldn't have to demand it. It's your responsibility, your obligation as a parent."

"I didn't want children."

Could the man really be so self-centered? "It's kind of late for that now. You know damned well what a paternity test will show. You can't deny your child's existence."

"Maybe not. But I plan to make sure Lauren doesn't get a penny more than what is necessary. I might wind up having to support the child, but I'm not going to support her." His gaze drifted over Gavin's suit. "Or some down-on-his-luck handyman who thinks he's found his ticket to the good life."

That capped it. Gavin's control snapped. He reached across the table and grabbed Holden by the lapels of his Armani jacket, yanking him half out of his seat. Coffee sloshed. Chair legs creaked. Gavin's lip curled back in a snarl.

"You son of a—"

"Go ahead, hit me," Holden coaxed. "Do it and I'll own that ramshackle house you call home as well as the surrounding acreage."

With an effort, Gavin reined in his temper. Beating the other man to a pulp, no matter how satisfying he would find the experience, wasn't going to help Lauren's situation. He released Holden and stood.

Around them, the other patrons were watching in fascination, their conversations apparently forgotten in the wake of the unexpected drama.

"You're going to regret that," Holden warned between gritted teeth as he smoothed down his lapels. "I might have been willing to let Lauren have some of our joint holdings. Now I'm going to fight her tooth and nail to keep them all. She's going to walk away from our marriage with nothing. Nothing!"

"And yet she'll still walk away," Gavin said. "What does that tell you?"

Lauren and the baby were well rid of him.

"Enjoy the good life while it lasts," Holden sneered.

Gavin meant it when he said, "I plan to."

* * *

He was too keyed up to drive back to Gabriel's Crossing. He needed to talk to someone. He needed advice. He knew where to find it: his brother.

Garrett was two years older than Gavin and half a head taller, but where Gavin was broad and more muscular, Garrett had a lean and rangy build, with longer arms and legs. In a fight—of which there had been plenty while they'd been growing up—they were evenly matched. In temperament, however, they were polar opposites, which is why they made good business partners.

Garrett was analytical, a details man. Where until recently Gavin had tended to move too quickly, Garrett took his time, sometimes too much time, gathering data and weighing facts before reaching a conclusion. Gavin needed his brother's thoughtful input today.

Garrett was in the conference room at Phoenix Brothers going over a set of blueprints with architects when Gavin walked in.

"This is a surprise. Has the prodigal returned?" He was only partly teasing.

"Don't, Garrett. Not today, okay?"

Garrett eyed him speculatively before turning to the other men. "Why don't you work on that revised materials quote and we'll finish this later." Once he and Gavin were alone, he said, "What's on your mind?"

Gavin shoved a hand through his hair and paced to the window. "I need some advice."

"Shoot."

"I just had a meeting with Lauren's husband. The jerk

is making the divorce ugly for her and as a result her blood pressure is up, which is a concern for the baby."

Garrett's brows crinkled. "Lauren? As in your tenant?"

"She's more than that. She and I are…friends, too." God! That word just kept coming up. The more he heard the description, the more he loathed it.

"Gav, look, I know you mean well. She's pregnant, needy and alone. It's only natural that you want to be there for her. But friend or no friend, this woman's divorce isn't any of your business."

"What if I want it to be?" he asked quietly.

Garrett flung his arms wide and swore. "Here we go again! Jeez, and this one isn't even single."

"What in the hell is that supposed to mean?"

"You're doing it again," Garrett accused. "Leaping without looking first. How many cliffs do you have to jump off before you figure out that you can't fly?"

"Lauren's not like Helena," he began.

But Garrett cut him off. "How would you know? You met her, what, a few months ago? She's married *and* pregnant, Gavin. Talk about baggage. At least Helena was just flighty and a flirt. Do yourself a favor—hell, do *me* a favor—and don't get involved."

"What do you mean, do you a favor?" Gavin demanded, his temper rising to match his brother's.

"I've picked up the slack here these past several months while I've waited for you to get your head together out in Connecticut. The name of our company is Phoenix Brothers Development." He slammed his fist down on the conference table for emphasis. "Brothers as in plural. But I've been a one-man show. We had to pass on a couple of good jobs as a result and our competitors were only too happy to land them."

Guilt settled in, taking the place of Gavin's anger. "You should have said something."

"I'm saying something now. I agreed when you said you needed to take a leave, Gav. How could I not? Hell, anybody with eyes could see that you needed one. You were no good to me, to the company, in that condition. But you promised—*promised*—that you'd get your head together and be back at least part-time by this spring. I can't afford for you to jump blindly into another doomed relationship that leaves you a useless husk when it ends."

"That's not what this is."

"Are you sure?" Garrett asked.

"I think so."

"That's not the same as sure." Garrett pinned him with a glare. "You need to be sure, *damned* sure. Because if we have to keep passing on the big jobs, our company could be on the line."

Gavin took his time driving home, and he mulled his brother's words the entire way. They weren't what he'd wanted to hear. Garrett wasn't right about Lauren or their situation. Lauren certainly wasn't a thing like his ex-wife. But he and Garrett had argued similarly when Gavin met Helena, and so his brother's words weighed on him.

* * *

It was nearly dinnertime when Lauren saw Gavin's car zip up the drive. She loved the cottage and the Connecticut countryside, but without someone to share them with their appeal had dimmed. She told herself she wasn't watching for Gavin or anticipating his return. But she was certainly glad when she spotted his car. Besides, she was curious about where he'd been for the better part of the day. He hadn't said anything about being gone, but when she'd gone to the house midmorning to bring him a pastry and talk him into taking a break, no one had been home.

After that, the rest of the day had been quiet and lonely, although Lauren had managed to be productive. She'd finally ordered a crib, changing table and dresser for the baby, as well as a bouncy seat and swing. Lilly had phoned just after she'd placed the order.

"Hey, leave something for your shower guests to purchase," her friend had teased. In the background Lauren could hear a toddler squealing.

Lauren had laughed politely, but said nothing.

"Your mother is throwing you a shower, isn't she?" Lilly had asked.

"She hasn't mentioned anything," Lauren had admitted. "In fact, we've only spoken twice in the past six weeks and both times she called to see if Holden and I had reconciled."

Lauren had accepted her mother's inability to act maternal. She credited Gavin for that. Blind, he'd said, making the deficiency out to be Camille's.

"That's it!" Lauren had just been able to make out

Lilly's muttered curses and hoped no small ears were within hearing distance. "I'm flying out and throwing you a shower."

"I'd love that. Really, Lil. But I know how busy you are with the kids. Besides, I don't really need a shower. I can afford to buy whatever the baby needs."

"I'm not that busy that I can't make time for one of my oldest and dearest friends," Lilly had countered. "And sure you can buy everything you need, but that's not really the point of those things, Lauren. Babies are to be celebrated."

She'd teared up at that. "I know. But who would I invite? My friends from the city would have to drive more than two hours to come. And I don't know that I can count on my mother to show up at all. I'd hate to seem pathetic."

"Leave the guest list to me. Just give me a date."

She had and then her friend said, "Now, tell me about this Gavin O'Donnell."

"Why do you ask about him?"

"Judging from the number of times his name has come up in our recent conversations and e-mails, it sounds like you have some pretty strong feelings for him."

The pause that had followed was as pregnant as Lauren.

"Still there?" Lilly had asked.

"Gavin and I are just friends." She'd rolled her eyes. How often was one or the other of them saying that?

"For now," Lilly had agreed. "But I think eventually the two of you will be much more than that."

Lilly's comment was still on Lauren's mind when

Gavin pulled into the driveway. The little thrill of excitement she felt at seeing him seemed to confirm her friend's assessment. And though she told herself to stay inside and go about her business, not even the threat of being photographed by someone Holden had hired could keep Lauren from bundling up in her coat, wrapping a scarf around her neck and walking out to the garage to greet him.

Leaves crunched underfoot as she approached and Gavin glanced over. He'd been scowling, lost in thought, but when he spied her, his expression brightened and he waved.

"Hello." Noting his business attire, she said, "I didn't realize you had a meeting today. Was it in the city?"

"Um, yeah." The Windsor knot at his collar had been loosened and the top button of his shirt unfastened. He tugged off the tie completely now and wadded it into a ball, which he stuffed into his pocket. He began to scowl again.

"It didn't go well, I take it," she said.

"No. Not like I'd hoped." He expelled a breath and Lauren waited for him to continue, but he didn't.

So, after a moment, she said, "I'm sorry."

"This isn't your fault. So, don't apologize, dammit!"

His near-shout almost had her backing away. The old Lauren probably would have. But meekness no longer suited her, if it ever had. She crossed her arms over her chest and stepped closer until he was within arm's reach. "I'm only being polite."

Gavin closed his eyes and sighed again. "Yes and I'm being insufferably rude."

"I don't know that I'd say 'insufferably,'" she replied.

He opened one eye and squinted at her. "Does that mean you forgive me?"

Lauren smiled. How could she not? He'd stood by her enough times. It felt good to finally be able to return the favor. "Want to talk about whatever it is that has put you in such a foul mood?"

He watched her intently before nodding slowly. "Yeah. I want to talk about it. In fact, we *need* to talk about it. It concerns you, Lauren."

Nerves skittered up her spine. "Me? How? I'm afraid I don't understand."

"I know." He tilted his head in the direction of the house. "Come inside. It's cold out here and you probably shouldn't be on your feet."

"I feel fine." But she followed him up the walk and through the rear door of the house just the same.

Inside the spacious kitchen, she felt instantly at home. She supposed it was because Gavin had allowed her such a free hand in decorating it. He'd picked oak cabinets originally. Those had come down and gone back after she'd mentioned a preference for maple. The light, hand-crafted cabinets contrasted nicely with the dark granite countertops.

Contrasts could be good, she thought. She and Gavin were different, but ultimately they complemented each other much like the room's furnishings.

Gavin took her coat and scarf and motioned for her to sit.

"Can I make you a cup of tea or something?" he asked.

Lauren shook her head. "Nothing for me, thanks."

He glanced at the clock. "I didn't realize it had gotten so late. Maybe I should start dinner."

"It's my turn to cook," she reminded him.

"Not today. You shouldn't be on your feet."

"So you keep saying. I'm not an invalid, Gavin."

"I know that, but I don't want to take any chances with you or the baby."

His concern touched her and helped take away some of the chill she was feeling. "Okay, I'll let you cook, but dinner can wait until after we've had our conversation."

"Right." He tucked his hands into his trouser pockets, scowling again, but said nothing.

"Gavin, you're starting to make me nervous."

"That's not my intention."

"I know. Come and sit," she coaxed, patting the tabletop. "Maybe it would be best if you just said whatever it is you want to say."

He nodded and shuffled over, sliding onto the chair opposite hers. "I went to see Holden today."

She'd told Gavin to blurt it out, but his words were a shock, so much so that she was sure she must have heard him wrong. "You what?"

"My meeting in the city today, it was with Holden."

"My husband asked to see you?"

Gavin cleared his throat. "Um, no. Actually, Lauren, I called him yesterday. I told him I wanted to talk to him."

"You called him," she repeated, her voice rising

slightly. "You called Holden and arranged a meeting with him without telling me?"

He nodded.

Her tone turned shrill when she went on. "You went to see him without asking me if I wanted or would appreciate your interference."

He squinted at her, looking both guilty and contrite. "Yes. I did that."

"Why?" she demanded. "Why on earth would you do something like that?"

"Because he's playing games with you." Gavin stood and paced to the far counter. He shoved a hand through his hair before he turned to face her. "You were so upset after he had you served with those papers. And then you came home from your doctor appointment and your blood pressure was up. What was I supposed to do, Lauren? Just sit back and let him tear you up inside? Don't ask me to do that. I can't."

His words warmed her heart. Still she said, "You might have asked me what *I* wanted, or at the very least you might have mentioned the meeting to me."

"I didn't want to upset you."

"Oh, please!"

Gavin continued, "But your blood pressure—"

"What, you don't think it's up now?"

When he blanched to nearly the same color as his snowy shirt, she almost took her words back, but anger simmered. It was an amazingly exhilarating emotion, Lauren decided, as was the give and take of her conversation with Gavin. She'd rarely experienced anything like it in the past, either with her parents or with her husband, and so she continued. "You went behind my back, Gavin."

"For your own good."

"No!" She slashed a hand through the air as she rose and went to him. "Don't treat me like a child. I'm tired of people telling me what to think, how to act and how to react. I'm sick *to death* of them making decisions for me. I'm quite capable of thinking for myself, you know." She said the words with a conviction she finally felt. Forget exhilarated. Lauren felt liberated, empowered.

"I know that."

"Good. Then start acting like you know that. This is my life, Gavin. It's my business." She tapped her chest with a finger for emphasis.

"You don't want me involved."

"I didn't say that." Her tone softened. "I want to be involved. Okay?"

He pulled her in for a hug. "*I* think I can manage that."

Afterward, as Lauren set the table and he prepared dinner, she asked, "So, what did you and Holden talk about?"

Gavin had gone the easy route: grilled cheese sandwiches and tomato soup. He concentrated on cooking as he relayed the high points of their conversation. He left out the part about grabbing Holden by the lapels.

"By the way, he thinks I'm a down-on-my-luck handyman and you're my sugar mama." He bobbed his eyebrows at her and grinned, hoping to lighten the moment.

Lauren gave an indelicate snort. "He can be such a small-minded snob at times. It's bad enough he's claiming we're having an affair."

Gavin flipped the sandwiches and lowered the heat on the soup. "You know, I've been giving that some thought. He's trying to use it as a bargaining chip in your divorce. Why not let him?"

She frowned. "I'm afraid I'm not following you."

"Under the previous grounds you were going to have to live separately for at least a year before a divorce could be granted under New York law," he reminded her.

"Go on."

"Well, with infidelity as the grounds, the timetable could be shortened."

"So, you think I should just let him make the claim?" she asked.

"I think you should *think* about it. I'm not going to make the mistake of telling you what to do." He held up the stainless steel spatula in surrender, still amazed at what a tigress lurked beneath her seemingly kitten exterior.

"I probably shouldn't admit this, but I enjoyed arguing with you," she said.

"Yeah?"

She glanced away. "Yeah."

Without thinking, he confessed, "It was kind of a turn-on." The words hung in the air between them, as ripe and as tempting as forbidden fruit. He cleared his throat as he felt the heat creep into his cheeks.

"I was going to say liberating," Lauren said.

"Ah." It was the only sound he was capable of making at the moment. God, he felt like an idiot.

"But I like your description, too," she said quietly.

He fiddled with the handle of the spatula, his gaze fixed on it rather than on her when he admitted, "I don't know if I'm supposed to say stuff like that about a pregnant woman."

"I'm a woman first, Gavin. And I won't always be pregnant."

The spatula clattered to the floor, dividing the space between them. He left it there.

Lauren went on. "I won't be married for much longer, either."

He looked up. She was smiling. "Especially, if I take your advice. Holden is claiming I've been unfaithful as a way to ensure he doesn't have to pay me alimony. But I don't want spousal support anyway."

"I told him as much. He seems to think you've grown accustomed to a certain standard of living and won't be able to do without it now."

She rolled her eyes. "Oh, I can do without it."

"I told him that, too."

"You know me far better than he does," she mused.

That was because he paid attention.

"I may wind up getting less than I could in the settlement," Lauren was saying. "But at least the process won't become a prolonged or protracted mess."

"There's that," he agreed.

"Of course, you did once tell me to be careful about giving up everything just to get the divorce over and done with."

"Yeah, I said that. But that was before…" Gavin stared at Lauren, unable to finish the sentence aloud.

Before what?

Before he'd realized what an utter imbecile her husband was?

Before he realized how upsetting the divorce was going to be for Lauren and the stress it would put on her unborn child?

Or was it before he'd realized that he was half in love with her and wanted her to be free as quickly as possible so he could pursue a relationship?

He took a step toward her, kicking the spatula. As it skittered across the floor, Gavin heard his brother's words from earlier in the day: *be damned sure.*

"Gavin, what is it?"

The smell of burning bread rescued him from saying more. He pulled the pan from the burner and waved a hand to disperse the smoke. "It looks like I'll have to start our sandwiches all over."

"You probably should lower the heat," she suggested with a simple smile that made his insides feel as if they were about to incinerate.

"Lower the heat." He repeated her advice with a

vigorous nod. Until he was sure exactly where their relationship was headed and where he wanted it to head, that was the wisest course for all parties involved.

CHAPTER TEN

GAVIN pulled the mail from the box at the road. In addition to the assortment of Christmas cards, a big manila envelope caught his eye. It was for Lauren, the return address the Shaw Advertising Agency in San Diego, California. He frowned.

He was still frowning when he reached her door.

"This came for you," he said, handing her the package after she ushered him inside.

She glanced at the label. "Lilly," she replied on a smile.

"Lilly's in advertising?"

"No. But her husband is friends with one of the top people at this agency. I guess he must have put in a good word for me."

"Are you thinking of applying?"

Gavin waited for her to say no. He wanted her to. California? It was on the other side of the country. Despite the conveniences of modern travel, it might as well have been on the other side of the galaxy.

Her reply was anything but reassuring. "I'm going to

need to get a job at some point after the baby comes. My savings won't last forever."

"But I thought you wanted to start your own agency?"

"I do. Maybe someday I will." She ran a hand over her distended belly. "But that's a pipe dream, Gavin. Pipe dreams don't pay the bills."

"Says who? It doesn't have to be a dream. My brother and I started out with nothing but big plans and egos to match. That's why banks grant people loans, to turn dreams into reality."

"You really believe in me."

It wasn't amazement he heard or gratitude, which he'd already made plain he didn't want. It was something bigger and went far deeper. Something that was binding them together. Strings, he thought. But he didn't try to untangle them.

"Yeah, I believe in you. You're smart, creative, organized." A dozen other adjectives came easily to mind. The woman was amazing. "You could do this."

She nodded. "Someday."

"Why not now?"

"Even assuming I could qualify for a loan, with the baby coming, I have neither the time nor the energy to devote to make it successful. Someday," she said again, sounding less wistful and more resolute.

"I'm going to hold you to that."

Lauren's contractions started just after midnight more than three weeks into the new year and just two days before her due date. The high blood pressure thankfully had proved to be stress induced, and the remainder of her pregnancy had been largely uneventful. Until the first cramping spasm sliced through her abdomen and forced her to curl into a ball beneath her bed's down comforter, she'd felt perfectly prepared to give birth. Indeed, she'd been eager to finally come face-to-face with the little person who had been using her bladder as a punching bag for these past months.

She'd picked out names: Will for a boy and Emily for a girl. She'd washed and sorted the gifts she'd received at the shower her friend Lilly had graciously flown out for and hosted. They'd had it at the farmhouse, in Gavin's much more spacious living room.

Lauren had been touched that several of her old co-workers had come, as well as a couple of neighbors from the apartment she'd shared with Holden. Her mother had not attended, no great surprise there. Camille had called with her regrets a week after the invitations went out. There was a conference in Salt Lake City that she *absolutely* had to attend, so she couldn't make it.

But Gavin's mother had. He'd invited her and she'd come, probably out of curiosity as much as out of courtesy. His sister, Grace, had attended with her. Lauren found both women to be interesting and delightful, even if they had plied her with questions that spelled out rather clearly their concern over Gavin's involvement with her.

As for that involvement it had remained rather

benign given the advanced state of her pregnancy and the slow pace of her divorce. They still ate meals together, talked and took walks when the weather allowed it. But he'd never again kissed her the way he had that day in the cottage.

The baby shower had been small but special. Lilly had seen to that with Gavin's help. The next evening, after Mrs. O'Donnell and Grace had gone home and Lilly had been dropped off at the airport, Gavin and Lauren had spent an hour going through the gifts she'd received. Gavin had oohed and ahhed right along with her when she'd held up tiny outfits, rattles and soft blankets. Then he'd insisted on helping her set up the crib and changing table that had been delivered a month earlier.

At the time, Lauren had felt perfectly calm when it came to impending motherhood. But now, as the hours passed and her contractions intensified, she began having second thoughts.

Major second thoughts.

"Oh, God! I don't think I can do this," she cried as another contraction began. Her panic built right along with the pain.

She tried the breathing technique she'd learned during her Lamaze classes. Gabriel's Crossing didn't have a hospital, so she'd been going to the one in nearby Danbury. A nurse on staff had agreed to act as Lauren's coach. She'd thought about asking Gavin, since he'd insisted he would drive her to the hospital when the time came, but modesty prevented her from doing so. She'd seen the childbirth video. It was an amazing thing, truly and utterly miraculous, but it was *not* the image she wanted seared into the brain of the man with whom she hoped to someday pursue a more-than-friends relationship.

She glanced out the window now. The drive to Danbury wasn't overly long, but the fact that it had snowed the night before did nothing to calm her already frayed nerves. A good three inches of the white stuff covered the walkway between the cottage and Gavin's back door, not that she felt up to walking the short distance at the moment anyway. She picked up the telephone and dialed his number. Gavin answered on the third ring.

"Hello?"

"Hi. It's Lauren." After saying that she hoisted the bottom of the receiver up to her forehead so she could pant without leaving Gavin to wonder if she was attempting to make an obscene phone call.

"Hey, Lauren. Great morning, huh? Have you looked outside yet?"

"Yes." *Hoo, hoo. Hee, hee.*

"It looks like a Currier & Ives print. The blue sky really sets it off."

"Hmm," was all she managed. Under other circumstances she would have agreed with him. But at the moment she didn't want slick roads standing between her and the epidural she'd been promised.

"I'm thinking of grabbing my camera and walking into the orchard to take some shots. Feel up for a walk after breakfast?" he asked.

"Not really." *Hoo-hoo. Hee-hee.*

She realized she'd breathed right into the receiver when he said, "Lauren, everything okay?"

"No. I'm ha-ha-having contractions."

"Now?" He sounded incredulous and almost as panicked as she felt, but he rallied valiantly. "Hang on, sweetheart, I'll be right there."

He was as good as his word. She'd barely replaced the telephone receiver in its cradle before she saw him flying out the back door of the farmhouse. He bolted down the snowy walkway coatless without his shoes.

"How are you doing?" he asked when he managed to catch his breath.

"Okay. Scared," she admitted. "I don't think I can do this."

"Sure you can, sweetheart."

That made twice now that he'd called her that. She'd never been anyone's sweetheart. Other than Borin' Lauren she'd never had a nickname. She rather liked the endearment, especially coming from Gavin.

"Women have babies all the time," he was saying. "There's no reason for you to be scared. None. All right?"

"All right." She let out a deep breath. His words weren't all that comforting, but his presence was. She felt safe with him. Over the past several months he'd showed her one thing: she could count on him.

"Do you have a bag packed?" he asked.

She waved a hand in the direction of the stairs. "It's in the bedroom closet."

"Great. Why don't you call the doctor while I go get it?" he suggested.

"Okay."

Lauren left a message with the doctor's service and then struggled into her coat. Gavin returned in time to help her on with her boots.

Kneeling in front of her, he said, "This probably isn't the best time to mention this, but I've got a serious thing for your ankles."

With her legs straight out, she could just see them over the mound of her belly. "They're swollen."

"I love them anyway." He dropped a light kiss on her left ankle and reached for her boot.

"My feet are swollen, too," she added as he tried to fit one foot into the supple leather. A thought struck her then. Oh, good God! It had been more than a week since she'd last shaved her legs. "I can't go to the hospital!" she hollered.

Gavin glanced up. "Yes, you can. You can do this," he repeated, misinterpreting her panic.

"No. You don't understand. I can't go to the hospital until I shave my legs."

"Lauren," he began in a patient voice.

But she was shaking her head. Suddenly, the most important thing in the world to her was to have perfectly smooth calves when she had to put her feet up in the stirrups and push. And so she announced defiantly, "I'm not going anywhere until I shave my legs."

"Okaaaay," he said on a sigh.

"I know you think I'm being ridiculous, but…" She let her words trail off. She *was* being ridiculous. Even knowing that, however, she wasn't about to change her mind. Everything else was outside her control at the moment. Stubble-free legs were not.

Gavin straightened and held out a hand to help her from the chair. "Just be quick about it so we can go."

Quick about it? It had been a major endeavor to shave them the last time. As she nibbled her lip, Gavin asked, "What are you waiting for?"

"You need to help me."

His mouth dropped open for a moment and he stared at her as if she'd really lost her mind this time. "You want me to shave your legs?"

"Please. It will take me forever." She patted her abdomen and stated the obvious, "I'm not quite as agile as I used to be. It's hard to bend over."

"Right." He nodded. "Do I have to shave your ankles, too?"

"Well, they are part of my legs." She smiled.

"You ask a lot."

"You can handle it," she assured him on a laugh. "My razor is in the shower and so is the shaving gel."

Gavin retrieved the items. When he turned around, Lauren was seated on the closed lid of the toilet seat attempting to roll up her pant legs.

"Let me get those," he offered, kneeling down.

After he put a towel on the floor under her feet, he slathered one leg with the shaving gel and got down to business. After several long, even strokes he'd completed the first one.

"You're pretty good at this," she said.

"Well, I've had a lot of practice."

Her eyebrows shot up at that.

"On my face," he clarified and they both laughed.

He retrieved a clean washcloth from inside the vanity and, after wetting it down, wiped the last of the gel from Lauren's leg. Then he started on the other one. Another time and under vastly different circumstances, performing this intimate chore for her could have been a highly erotic experience, especially as the razor head toured her slim ankles. He filed it away for future reference. He definitely wanted to try it again someday.

After finishing up he dried off her legs, helped her into a pair of socks and rolled down her pants. "Need a haircut before we go? Maybe a perm?" he asked wryly.

"Ha, ha. Very funny." She pulled a face that had him grinning.

Gavin was glad to see some of the fear and panic had ebbed from her expression. The doctor called back then with questions. How long had she been having contractions? How frequent were they? After she hung up, she said, "Well, he says it's a go."

"Okay. What do you say we get your boots and coat and be on our way?"

Lauren nodded, and he could tell by the way she had started to breathe through her mouth that another contraction was beginning to mount. The sooner they were on the road the better, he decided. He grabbed her suitcase and opened the cottage door, but she stopped walking and wouldn't budge. She just stood in the doorway, one arm braced on the jamb, panting as if she'd just run a marathon.

"What is it? Is it the baby?" The image of having to deliver her child himself popped into his head and had the blood draining out of it. He felt a little woozy at the prospect, but he'd do it. He would do whatever was necessary to keep Lauren and her baby safe.

"Not…the…baby," she finally managed. "You."

"Me?"

She motioned toward his feet. "You might… want… to put on some shoes."

"Shoes." Gavin glanced down at his feet. He wore only a pair of navy socks that were soggy from his trek through the snow. He smiled sheepishly. "Yeah. That would probably be a good idea."

"And…a coat."

"Right." He laughed. "Guess I wasn't thinking."

Lauren's contraction was over and from her expression he could tell that some of her apprehension was returning. "Are you nervous, too?" she asked.

Nervous, scared and half a dozen other things. But Gavin pasted a grin on his face, shook his head and reached for her hand.

"Nah. I'm excited. I'm going to meet my second-favorite girl today."

Or maybe not, he realized. At the hospital, Lauren's

labor continued throughout the afternoon. By evening she was exhausted and Gavin was, too. He'd stayed by her side in the labor room, rubbing her back and feeding her ice chips. Early into the process, he'd learned the hard way not to offer her a hand to hold when a contraction came. Lauren had never struck him as a physically strong woman, but when her fingers had curled around his in a crushing, viselike grip, it was all he could do not to whimper and fall to his knees.

After she'd let go he'd half teased, "Was that so you could share a little bit of the pain?"

She'd glanced at him in confusion. "What?"

"Nothing." He'd given his hand a discreet shake, hoping to restore the circulation.

Just before seven o'clock the doctor came in and checked on her progress. Gavin busied himself plumping up her pillows during the exam, feeling conspicuous and a little awkward.

"It will be a while yet. Why don't you take a stroll around the halls," the doctor suggested, nixing plans for an epidural. "I'll be back in an hour, and hopefully things will be progressing by then."

So, they walked the halls in the hopes that would speed up the delivery. But when the doctor checked back around nine, Lauren's cervix had dilated only another half centimeter. It was looking to be a very long night. The baby's vital signs were being monitored carefully and the doctor didn't appear overly concerned. But Gavin was. He pulled one of the nurses aside.

"How much longer is it going to be? Lauren's endured enough. I don't know how much more of this she can take." Or how much more he could handle. It was absolute hell watching her writhe in pain and not be able to do a damned thing to help her.

The woman smiled sympathetically and patted his hand. "It could be another hour or two or even three. It's hard to say. Babies make their own schedules. But don't worry. Your wife is doing fine. Just fine. And your son or daughter will be here before you know it."

Wife.

Son or daughter.

The words made Gavin yearn, so much so that he didn't bother to correct her. He wanted what the nurse assumed he already had. He wanted Lauren as his wife. He wanted her child to be his child, even if not biologically. Eventually, he promised himself, eventually he would have them. They would be a family.

Half in love with her? Nope. He'd fallen all the way without ever taking her out on a real date. Without ever doing more than hold her hand, stroke her back, kiss her lips. This was different than it had been with Helena, but he was still going to take his time. Lauren needed to settle in to motherhood and there was the not so small matter of her husband still being in the picture. She'd been hurt, emotionally mistreated by both Holden and her parents. She'd come a long way already, but he wanted all of her wounds to heal, just as his had thanks in large part to her.

In the meantime, he had plans to make for their future.

* * *

It was nearly midnight before Lauren's cervix was finally fully dilated and she was ready to begin pushing. Gavin had gone to the waiting room. She'd requested that, but then found herself longing for his presence in those final moments before she gave birth. It wasn't that she relied on him, she realized. She loved him.

I love Gavin.

She'd picked one heck of a time to have such an epiphany. She was moments away from motherhood and months away from being single again. But as she bore down for the final time, she didn't doubt the sentiment's truth. She'd loved him since he'd bought that ridiculous teddy bear, maybe even before. He'd shown her so many small acts of kindness over the months, little things that had kept adding up until her heart simply spilled over.

"It's a girl," the doctor said, holding up a squalling bundle for Lauren to see.

A girl. Just as Gavin had said it would be. Through the haze of her tears she could make out a set of flailing arms and a blotchy, scrunched-up face that already owned her heart. She laughed a little before sobbing hysterically.

"My Emily," she whispered. Here was her daughter. Here, at last, was the miracle she'd been expecting. Could it be that another one was out in the waiting room?

A little later, once Lauren had been moved to a private room with the baby, she turned to the nurse.

"Can you go and find Gavin O'Donnell for me and tell him that he was right? He knew all along that the baby was going to be a girl."

The nurse nodded. "Sure. I'll tell him. Or you could tell him yourself. Would you like me to ask him to come in? I have it on pretty good authority that he's been pacing around the waiting room like a caged tiger since he left your side. He's driving the folks at the nurses' station crazy."

Lauren wanted to see Gavin more than anything, but she raised a hand to her matted hair and grimaced. "How do I look?"

"You look like you just gave birth to a beautiful and healthy baby girl. You're lovely." The nurse smiled then. "All new mothers are lovely."

That probably meant Lauren looked a wreck, but excitement trumped vanity in this instance. "Okay. I'd appreciate it if you'd send him in."

A few minutes later Gavin poked his head around the door before coming fully inside. His face was haggard, shadowed by a day's growth of beard. Worry lines creased his forehead, and his eyes were seriously bloodshot. Her heart somersaulted at the sight of him. Oh, yes, she loved him.

"Hi, Mommy."

"That's me." She grinned.

"The nurse said you had someone you wanted me to meet."

"I do indeed." She held out a hand to him, urging him

closer when it seemed like he would linger in the doorway. "This is Emily."

"Emily, huh?" Gavin's grin spread as he crossed to the bed. "I told you the baby was a girl."

"Yes, you did."

His expression softened as he peered at the tiny face. The baby was wrapped in a striped pastel blanket and wearing a little pink hat. She was sound asleep, a condition the nurse had assured Lauren was not likely to last long.

"God, Lauren, she's beautiful." His tone was low, reverent. "But then I knew she would be. She looks just like you."

"Her eyes are blue when they're open, and she has hair, too." Lauren removed the small cap to reveal a downy, sable-colored thatch that stuck straight up on the top of the baby's head.

"That's some 'do." He chuckled. "She has your chin." He touched it with the tip of his index finger and even though Emily was sleeping one side of her mouth lifted almost as if she knew who he was. "Did you see that? I think she smiled."

His delight was endearing.

"Would you like to hold her?" she asked.

Dimples creased his cheeks as he smiled. "Are you kidding? I can't think of anything I want to do more at the moment."

He scooped the baby up in his hands, taking care to support Emily's neck and head. Lauren had seen the man wield power tools and sledgehammers. He looked equally at home now holding a newborn. As he settled her into the crook of his arm, he lowered himself onto the edge of Lauren's bed.

"What does she weigh? She feels as light as a feather."

"Seven pounds, eleven ounces."

"That's pretty respectable," he said, his gaze never straying from Emily's face. Then he pulled back the blanket and held a pair of tiny pink feet in the palm of his hand. "All her piggies are accounted for, I see."

"Yes."

"You do good work."

All the emotional uncertainty of the past several months, all of the physical pain of the past several hours, none of it mattered any longer. "She's a keeper," Lauren agreed on a sigh.

"Both of you are." He leaned down and pressed a kiss to her forehead. "How are you feeling? It's been a long day and an even longer night."

"I'm exhausted and sore," she admitted. "And wide awake. I should be sleeping. Isn't that the first rule of motherhood? Grab sleep whenever you can? But I don't want to close my eyes. I'm afraid if I do I'll wake up back at the cottage and Emily's birth will have been just a dream."

"She's real, Lauren, and she's here."

"And you?"

"What do you mean?" he asked.

Emotions tumbled. "Are you real, too?" she asked quietly.

He smiled, almost as if he understood the strange question. "Uh-huh. And I'm not going anywhere, either. So, close your eyes and sleep."

She did. With Gavin sitting at her bedside holding her newly born daughter, Lauren closed her eyes and allowed herself to slip into a peaceful slumber.

CHAPTER ELEVEN

IT BECAME a habit, falling asleep while Gavin stood watch over Emily. For the next several weeks, as Lauren tried to get the baby on some sort of schedule, about the only thing she could count on was that right about the time she'd reached her limit—either emotionally or physically—Gavin would be there, ready to lend a hand or take over completely while she took a nap or showered or grabbed a bite to eat. The only time she was on her own was late at night. Even then she knew if she needed him, all she had to do was pick up the phone and call.

The week after Emily's birth, Lauren's parents came out to see their only grandchild. They stayed at a bed-and-breakfast in Gabriel's Crossing and complained mightily about everything during their stay, which thankfully was brief. Three days of their self-absorbed sniping was more than enough for Lauren.

The only bright spot of their visit was that they seemed genuinely thrilled about Emily. They didn't exactly dote over the baby. Camille and Dwight weren't that type. But they did seem interested, which Lauren appreciated. Of course, both of her parents took the opportunity to again lecture her about leaving Holden, but apparently they'd accepted that Lauren wasn't going to change her mind.

When they met Gavin, they were cordial but not overly friendly. Like Holden, they took Gavin at face value, seeing only what he presented, a working-class man who was good with his hands. They would have been impressed had they been privy to the scope of his accomplishments. She saw no reason to enlighten them.

As for Holden, he hadn't seen the baby. Lauren had called him from the hospital to tell him of Emily's birth. She hadn't really wanted to speak to him, but she'd figured, as the baby's father, he had a right to know. He'd asked the pertinent questions—how much did the baby weigh, was she healthy. Beyond that he hadn't seemed overly interested. At least he hadn't mentioned the DNA test. She'd hung up feeling sad for Emily and yet relieved that in the long run Holden wasn't going to be part of the picture. Holden might not want their daughter, but Lauren knew someone who did.

Gavin absolutely adored Emily, and, as winter gave way to spring, the feeling appeared to be mutual. Whenever he peeked over the side of the crib, the baby smiled and waved her small fists in excitement. Like Lauren, she knew she could count on him, too.

In so many ways, Lauren, Gavin and Emily were like a family. Yes, they were *like* a family, and often mistaken for one when they were out, but they were not a family. Just as Lauren and Gavin were like a couple in many regards—sharing evening meals and doting over the baby before Em went down for the night. But they were not a couple.

They were individuals, with separate concerns and objectives, as became clear when Gavin started back to work in Manhattan in late April. He'd made a commitment to his brother. He had an obligation to his company. Lauren understood that. Just as she understood that he'd made no commitment and had no obligation to her.

She assumed they had a future together. At times she felt certain that marriage was what Gavin wanted. *When the time and the woman are right*, he'd said. Of course, the time was far from perfect. But as her divorce inched toward being final, the subject had yet to come up. Now, with her savings dwindling and expenses mounting, Lauren reached a conclusion: she needed to get serious about finding a job.

She mentioned it to Gavin when he came by just after sunup one morning. He'd started stopping in for breakfast before his long commute to Manhattan. Some days, if traffic was heavy or he had to stay late in the city, the morning was the only time she saw him.

She missed their dinners together, their long conversations. She missed him, especially since he spent a good portion of the weekends working in the farmhouse. The renovations were close to being finished and he was no longer doing them alone. He'd hired a three-man crew to scrape and paint the exterior and detached garage, which got a new electric door, and a landscaper had already picked out the perennials and shrubs for the flower beds.

She could all but see the For Sale sign on the front lawn. What then? Lauren opted not to ask the question. Instead, as he fed Emily her bottle, she said, "I've decided to begin my job hunt in earnest."

Gavin glanced up sharply. "So soon?"

"Emily's nearly four months old. I've had a lot more time off than most new mothers." Still, her heart ached. She was hardly sold on the idea of leaving her daughter in someone else's care.

"So, where are you thinking of looking?" He pulled the bottle from the baby's mouth and brought her up to his shoulder to be burped. Lauren watched his big, work-roughened hands pat her daughter's back.

"I've got a few leads." She named off the agencies. She'd already updated her résumé and portfolio. Both were ready to be popped in the mail.

He nodded. "Manhattan, good."

She swallowed. "Of course, Lilly's still pulling for San Diego." Her friend had mentioned it again in their last conversation.

His hand stilled. "Would you consider that?"

"I don't know," she answered truthfully. "Lilly's offered to watch the baby for me while I'm at work."

That was the upside of the arrangement. Emily would be cared for by someone Lauren knew and trusted. The downside was sitting directly across from her. How could she leave the man she loved?

"Don't make any decisions yet."

"At some point I'll have to."

"I know. But not yet." He kissed the baby's head, the gesture as tender as it was second nature. "Promise me you'll wait."

She promised, but it struck her later that Gavin had never said what she was waiting for.

When Gavin couldn't make it to Gabriel's Crossing in time for dinner, he always called. The phone rang just as Lauren put the baby in her carrier seat and prepared to go grocery shopping.

"Hey, Lauren. It's me."

"You won't be home," she guessed on a sigh.

"No. Sorry. Something's come up." Something had been coming up a lot lately. "Hope you didn't take anything out for dinner."

She made a mental note to put the pork chops back in the freezer before they had a chance to completely thaw. "No. Don't worry. I know your schedule can be unpredictable."

"It won't always be." It sounded like a promise. "I'm working on something important at the moment. Something huge."

She smiled at the enthusiasm in his voice, knowing how much he loved what he did. "Want to tell me about it?"

"Yeah, I do. More than you can imagine. But I can't

just yet, Lauren." Curiosity tempered her disappointment when he added, "I want it to be a surprise."

Lauren lay awake in her bed even as Emily slept, snoring softly in her crib. She heard Gavin's car come up the driveway. The light from its high beams illuminated her room for a moment before darkness prevailed. She glanced at the clock on the nightstand. It was after eleven and he was just getting home. She rolled over, thinking that now maybe she would be able to drift off to sleep, but a light tapping sounded at her door.

Pulling on a robe, she went downstairs, flipping on a lamp on her way to answer the knock.

Gavin stood on the opposite side, as she'd known he would. He looked exhausted. His jaw was shadowed, eyes bloodshot. His tailored shirt was wrinkled from the long day and the long drive.

He was a sight for sore eyes. Lauren smiled as she moved in to wrap him in a hug.

"I like coming home to that," he sighed.

"I like having you come home." She felt his arms tighten around her waist, and he whispered something that she swore sounded like "soon."

"I have some pinot grigio in the fridge," she said after a moment, stepping back so he could come inside. "We can sit on the couch, talk. You can tell me about your day."

She started for the kitchen, but as she moved past him, Gavin snagged her hand and pulled her back.

Their bodies bumped. He settled his hands on her hips to keep her there.

"The wine can wait, so can the conversation. Ah, Lauren." He breathed her name into her hair before pushing it aside and nuzzling her neck. She welcomed the intimate contact, reveled in the sensations that showered through her like fireworks.

She found his mouth with hers, eager and greedy for more. It had been a long time. So very long. Need made her bold. She stroked his tongue, nipped his lower lip with her teeth. A moan vibrated from the back of his throat and his hands were no longer anchored to her waist. They'd left their safe moorings to part her robe. He pushed it off her shoulders. Rough palms snagged on the silky fabric of her nightgown, but then Gavin was lifting it, pulling it over her head.

Lauren knew a moment of self-consciousness as she stood before him naked except for a pair of panties. She was almost back to her prebaby weight, but the experience of childbirth had permanently altered parts of her anatomy. Her waist was thicker than it used to be, the skin on her abdomen no longer quite as taut.

Heat suffused her face. "Gavin, I'm—"

Shaking his head, he placed a fingertip against her lips. "You're beautiful, Lauren. Absolutely beautiful."

He made her *feel* beautiful and so her confidence returned, boldness racing neck and neck with desire. She reached for his shirt, unfastening the buttons and letting her lips follow her hands' progress. His shirt joined her clothes on the floor, and Gavin moaned.

She was reaching for his belt when Emily started to cry.

"I forgot we had company there for a minute." He laughed as he said it, but then blew out a deep breath.

Lauren did the same as she scooped up her robe and shrugged into it.

"I'll just be a minute. Ten tops. Help yourself to that wine and pour me a glass while you're at it." She started for the stairs, but then turned. "Don't go anywhere, Gavin, okay?"

He smiled. "I wouldn't dream of it. I'll be here."

And he was. Half an hour later, after Emily finally drifted off again, Lauren found Gavin on the couch. Two glasses of wine were on the low table in front of him. He was shirtless, shoeless and sound asleep.

But he'd kept his promise. He was there.

She wiggled onto the small strip of couch in front of him, resting her head on the corner of the throw pillow he'd commandeered. Though he didn't wake, his arm came around her, protective even in sleep.

"I love you," she whispered as she drifted off.

Gavin woke just before dawn, not completely sure where he was, although he knew perfectly well who was sleeping beside him.

He levered up on one elbow, careful not to disturb her. Lauren mumbled something and burrowed against his bare chest. The heart inside it took a tumble. This was what he wanted, *exactly* what he wanted, for the rest of his life. He'd known it with certainty since Emily's birth, of course, but he'd been biding his time, setting his plans in motion. He'd thought everything out carefully.

The farmhouse was nearly complete and he would be moving back to his apartment, but he had no intention of putting the property up for sale. Nor did he have any intention of living in Manhattan without Lauren and Emily. He'd been working on the guest room there, converting it to a nursery. He had similar plans for one of the rooms in the farmhouse, which they would enjoy as a weekend retreat.

He was going to ask Lauren to marry him. He already had the ring. He was just waiting for her divorce to become final. He leaned down and brushed a kiss over her temple. Last night, if he hadn't fallen asleep, they would have made love. Just thinking of it now had desire stirring. He blew out a breath and reeled in his desire. Maybe it was for the best that they hadn't. They'd waited this long. They could wait till she was legally single again. Till Emily was safely tucked into the care of a trusted sitter. He wanted it to be perfect. Lauren deserved nothing less.

She rolled, shifting to her other side. Her bottom pressed against his front. Gavin closed his eyes on a groan. A moment later, he eased out from behind her, cursing his carefully constructed plans but opting to avoid further temptation.

CHAPTER TWELVE

ON A RAINY Monday in June, Lauren's divorce became final. She went to the courthouse alone except for her lawyer. She hadn't wanted Gavin present and she'd seen no need to bring Emily. Holden hadn't asked to see his daughter.

When the judge made his ruling, Lauren felt no over-whelming emotion, unless one counted relief. It was a surreal moment, staring at the man she'd married, the man who had fathered her child, and realizing their paths weren't likely to cross often in the future, if ever, despite the visitation order that had been worked out.

The proceedings had included few surprises. Holden got to keep the apartment, its furnishings and some of their other real estate holdings, although he'd had to pay her a lump sum for the privilege. It wasn't an overly large amount. In fact, Lauren's lawyer had urged her to seek more. But she'd been afraid doing so would drag out the inevitable and she'd just wanted this done.

Besides, she had plenty to live on. Their joint bank

accounts and investments had been divided equitably, and though Lauren had refused alimony, she would be receiving monthly child support payments for Emily. Holden had also dropped his nonsensical DNA request and agreed to set up a college fund for his daughter.

The daughter whom he had yet to see.

The court granted Lauren sole custody. No surprise there since Holden hadn't wanted to share it and the distance between their current accommodations would have made that difficult anyway. Visitation was set. He was entitled to every third weekend and alternating holidays. Lauren wasn't overly concerned by the arrangement. It had already become abundantly clear that he wouldn't exercise the privilege.

At nearly six months old, Emily had just last week cut her first tooth. She babbled happily, smiled often and had an irresistible laugh. She was beautiful, bright and alert. She was the light of her mother's life. The fact that Holden chose not to share in it was his loss.

Lauren had forgotten her umbrella, and the rain was coming down harder. People dashed past her on the sidewalk, the unlucky ones holding soggy newspapers over their heads. She glanced up at the gray sky with its heavy, hanging clouds and smiled. It was sunny and fair as far as she was concerned.

She pulled out her cell phone and punched in Gavin's number, feeling ready to burst before he finally answered. "Hello?"

"Hi," she said.

"All done?"

"Yes. I just left court and I'm out for a stroll."

"It's pouring rain."

She laughed. "What are you talking about? It's a gorgeous day. I'm a single woman again."

"Single, huh? Well, then I've got a question for you."

Lauren laid a hand over her thumping heart. "Yes?"

"How about a date tonight?"

It wasn't quite the question she'd been hoping he'd ask, but even that didn't dim her happiness. "Sounds wonderful."

Gavin made plans to take Lauren to dinner in Midtown that evening to celebrate. He'd enlisted Garrett and his girlfriend, Amanda to babysit Emily while he and Lauren were out. On a date. Their *first* date, for all practical purposes.

They'd done things a little backward—eating meals and spending quiet evenings together, and of course sharing the birth of a child. But with the exception of a couple of steamy interludes, they hadn't done the things most couples do at the beginning. He planned to rectify that later tonight.

With that in mind, he'd run out to pick up a bottle of champagne. He was putting it on ice for later when Lauren walked into the living room. One look at her and Gavin wished he could fast-forward through the evening he had so carefully planned. He'd never seen her look quite like this, overtly sexy to the point his tongue wanted to loll out of his gaping mouth. He snapped his mouth closed and swallowed a moan.

The dress was a good deal more revealing than any she'd worn in the past, but that wasn't it. She looked confident, determined, as though she knew what she wanted and she knew how to get it. She walked toward him, letting her fingertips trail lightly over the back of the couch.

"I'm ready," she said.

So was he. More than, he thought.

Lauren hadn't worn high heels in months, but she had a pair on now, the strappy black variety that did incredible things for her already shapely calves and delectable ankles.

"You don't play fair," he murmured in appreciation.

"Nope. I play for keeps. While you were gone Cindy came by."

"Cindy?"

"I used to work with her. You met her at the shower. I took the liberty of calling her and asking a favor."

His brain wasn't working. In fact, the closer she came, the harder it was to think. "Favor?" he repeated.

Lauren moved slowly, her gaze locked on his. When she reached him, she settled her palms on his lapels. "I asked her to take Em for a few hours."

"But Garrett and Amanda—"

"I called them, too. Let them know of the change of plans. I had an interesting talk with your brother by the way."

"Hmm?" Her fingers had walked up his chest and were now teasing the hair at the back of his neck.

"He gave me what I consider a compliment, though maybe you can clarify it for me. He said it appeared that your cliff-jumping days were over. He credited me." She kissed his neck, nibbled on his ear before whispering. "Care to explain?"

Gavin pulled her flush against him, eager to return the sweet torture to which she'd just subjected him. "Sure, but not right now. That can wait. This can't."

He kissed her thoroughly and then swung her up in his arms, carrying her past the guest room where her things were stowed, to the master suite. She wouldn't be sleeping down the hall this night.

"I was wondering if we'd ever be alone together like this. It's been hell waiting."

"We didn't need to."

"I felt we did. Timing," he murmured as they helped one another undress. He took his time taking off her sandals, indulging at last in a feast of her ankles.

She moaned softly and then scooted farther back on the bed, until her head rested on the pillows. He followed her.

They made love with the lights on, watching each other's expressions and anticipating each other's needs as passion built and release beckoned.

Gavin waited till the aftershocks had ebbed before he said, "I love you, Lauren."

"I love you, too." She rolled onto her side so she could face him. "You mentioned timing earlier. So the time is right?"

His brow crinkled. "Uh-huh."

"And the woman. Am I right, too?" She was grinning.

He knew where she was heading. Damn, she was stealing his thunder and ruining his surprise.

"You're getting ahead of yourself," he warned.

"No, you've been falling behind. You need to catch up."

"I haven't wanted to rush things," he said.

"I appreciated that…at first. I can admit it made sense given my divorce. But here's the deal, my lease is up soon. I need to find a new place for me and Em to live, and I've got to decide on a job. I've had an offer." She sat up, not bothering to cover herself. "Actually, I've had two."

He sat up as well. "Why didn't you say something?"

"It just happened yesterday and I haven't made any decisions. One agency is in Manhattan."

"And the other one?"

"I think you know where it is. So?" Her lips twitched with the beginnings of a smile.

"Are you playing hardball with me?"

He expected her to deny it, but she grinned. "Yes, I am."

Self-confidence looked so good on her that Gavin couldn't work up to being offended. Still, he wasn't going to let her completely botch all of his meticulously laid plans.

"Well, I've got an offer for you, too." He stood and pulled on his pants. Then he tossed his shirt at her. "Put this on and follow me."

Lauren was baffled. A minute ago she'd been steering him toward matrimony and now she was being led

around the apartment in his shirt. What had happened?
She'd been sure he'd been about to propose. He loved
her. He loved her daughter. Her divorce was final. But
now he was giving her a tour of his home, even though
she'd already seen most of the rooms before.

"The office is one of my favorite rooms. There's a
great view from the window and plenty of cabinet space
for files. When you start your business—if that's what
you decide you want to do—you could work from here
if you'd like. That way you wouldn't have to be away
from Emily all day. We could bring a sitter in."

Lauren blinked. "Gavin."

"No, no. Don't say anything now. Just wait." With a
hand on her lower back, he steered her to the next room.

The door was closed. Before he turned the knob, he
said, "We can redo this if you don't like it, but I
couldn't resist."

He shoved the door open and Lauren gasped. The
room was painted pink and already furnished with a crib,
changing table and dresser. In the corner was a comfy
rocker. A tutu-wearing teddy bear similar to the one he'd
purchased so long ago was seated on its cushion.

"It was kind of my inspiration, so I bought a second
one," he said when he noticed where she was staring.
She realized then that the wallpaper border sported a
similarly clad stuffed animal. "We can keep the original
bear and your furniture in the nursery at the farmhouse.
I'll leave that one for you to decorate."

Lauren glanced around the room again, noting all of

the little details, like a night-light and diaper pail, even a wipes warmer on the changing table. "When did you find time to do all this?"

"Those late nights," he said on a shrug. "I wanted everything ready so that when the time was right I could ask you a certain question."

Her eyes filled with tears. "Oh, Gavin."

He'd thought of everything. Planning, plotting, taking his time where he'd once rushed so blindly ahead.

His eyes were bright, too, when he said, "Lauren, I love you. I have for a long time. I love Em, too. In fact, I have since before I saw her because she was part of you."

"We love you, too." She brushed tears from her cheeks.

"I want us to be a family," he said and more tears fell. He blotted them away this time. "Marry me, Lauren. I promise I'll make you happy."

"You already have."

She went into his arms, eager to be there, never wanting to leave them. And when he kissed her, Lauren knew, the future they'd both been busy planning had finally begun.

EPILOGUE

GAVIN grabbed two glasses of champagne from a waiter's tray and started through the crowd in search of Lauren. The artwork on display had earned rave reviews from those in attendance at the gallery opening, but in Lauren and Gavin's case, it wasn't the real draw. They'd needed a night out. They hadn't managed to do anything alone or remotely romantic since the birth of their son, Will, more than four months earlier.

He spied Lauren across the room and felt the familiar kick of attraction. Two years of marriage and it showed no signs of abating. She saw him, smiled, and he knew it was mutual.

She'd gotten her figure back since the baby, though she still complained that certain clothes no longer fit they way they had. He'd told her to buy new clothes. He loved her just the way she was.

And she was lovely. On this night she was wearing a basic black sheath with her blond hair up in a sleek twist accented with diamonds. No one in the room would have guessed that earlier in the day she'd been dressed in khakis, her hair down and one side adorned with little Will's regurgitated formula.

"Here you are." He held out one of the glasses for her and had just taken a sip of his own when he spied her ex. Holden was sneering, and a buxom brunette was hanging on his arm.

"This is a surprise," Holden said. "I was under the impression that this opening was by invitation only."

"Holden." Lauren's tone held a warning.

Not surprisingly, the man ignored her. Turning to Gavin, he said, "I wouldn't think this sort of thing would appeal to someone like you, O'Donnell. But then Lauren knows quite a bit about art. I'm sure she can explain the finer points of the medium to you."

"For your information…" Lauren began.

But Gavin shook his head. "Don't. It's okay. Come on."

They were just stepping away when Holden said in a stage whisper, "That's real champagne, by the way. Apparently one of the artist's patrons doesn't believe in sparing any expense. I hear he made his fortune in real estate."

"Yeah," Lauren agreed. "He's loaded, though you'd never know it from the way he acts. He's not the sort to flaunt it. He's classy." She smiled at Gavin, sipped the bubbling beverage. "Handsome. And incredibly sexy."

Holden frowned. "Wait a minute…" he began.

But Gavin had taken Lauren's arm and was steering

her away. "Sorry, can't," she called over her shoulder. "My husband and I are late for another engagement."

Outside Gavin pulled her into his arms, laughing even as he kissed her. Lifting his head, he said, "That was really bad of you, Mrs. O'Donnell."

"Just setting the record straight." Then Lauren grabbed his tie. Using it to tug him toward their waiting limousine, she added, "Now, if you want to see bad…"

* * * * *

Look for LAST WOLF WATCHING
by Rhyannon Byrd—the exciting conclusion in the
BLOODRUNNERS *miniseries*
from Silhouette Nocturne.

Follow Michaela and Brody on their fierce journey to
find the truth and face the demons from the past, as
they reach the heart of the battle between the Runners
and the rogues.

Here is a sneak preview of book three,
LAST WOLF WATCHING.

Michaela squinted, struggling to see through the impenetrable darkness. Everyone looked toward the Elders, but she knew Brody Carter still watched her. Michaela could feel the power of his gaze. Its heat. Its strength. And something that felt strangely like anger, though he had no reason to have any emotion toward her. Strangers from different worlds, brought together beneath the heavy silver moon on a night made for hell itself. That was their only connection.

The second she finished that thought, she knew it was a lie. But she couldn't deal with it now. Not tonight. Not when her whole world balanced on the edge of destruction.

Willing her backbone to keep her upright, Michaela Doucet focused on the towering blaze of a roaring bonfire that rose from the far side of the clearing, its orange flames burning with maniacal zeal against the inky black curtain of the night. Many of the Lycans had already shifted into their preternatural shapes, their fur-covered bodies standing like monstrous shadows at the edges of the forest as they waited with restless expectancy for her brother.

Her nineteen-year-old brother, Max, had been attacked by a rogue werewolf—a Lycan who preyed upon humans for food. Max had been bitten in the attack, which meant he was no longer human, but a breed of creature that existed between the two worlds of man and beast, much like the Bloodrunners themselves.

The Elders parted, and two hulking shapes emerged from the trees. In their wolf forms, the Lycans stood over seven feet tall, their legs bent at an odd angle as they stalked forward. They each held a thick chain that had been wound around their inside wrists, the twin lengths leading back into the shadows. The Lycans had taken no more than a few steps when they jerked on the chains, and her brother appeared.

Bound like an animal.

Biting at her trembling lower lip, she glanced left, then right, surprised to see that others had joined her. Now the Bloodrunners and their family and friends stood as a united force against the Silvercrest pack, which had yet to accept the fact that something sinister was eating away at its foundation—something that would rip down the protective walls that separated their world from the humans'. It occurred to Michaela that loyalties were being announced tonight—a separation made between those who would stand with the Runners in their fight against the rogues and those who blindly supported the pack's refusal to face reality. But all she could focus on was her brother. Max looked so hurt...so terrified.

"Leave him alone," she screamed, her soft-soled, black satin slip-ons struggling for purchase in the damp earth as she rushed toward Max, only to find herself lifted off the ground when a hard, heavily muscled arm clamped around her waist from behind, pulling her clear off her feet. "Damn it, let me down!" she snarled, unable to take her eyes off her brother as the golden-eyed Lycan kicked him.

Mindless with heartache and rage, Michaela clawed at the arm holding her, kicking her heels against whatever part of her captor's legs she could reach. "Stop it," a deep, husky voice grunted in her ear. "You're not helping him by losing it. I give you my word he'll survive the ceremony, but you have to keep it together."

"Nooooo!" she screamed, too hysterical to listen to reason. "You're monsters! All of you! Look what you've done to him! How dare you! *How dare you!*"

The arm tightened with a powerful flex of muscle, cinching her waist. Her breath sucked in on a sharp, wailing gasp.

"Shut up before you get both yourself and your brother killed. I will *not* let that happen. Do you understand me?" her captor growled, shaking her so hard that her teeth clicked together. "Do you understand me, Doucet?"

"Damn it," she cried, stricken as she watched one of the guards grab Max by his hair. Around them Lycans huffed and growled as they watched the spectacle, while others outright howled for the show to begin.

"That's enough!" the voice seethed in her ear. "They'll tear you apart before you even reach him, and I'll be damned if I'm going to stand here and watch you die."

Suddenly, through the haze of fear and agony and outrage in her mind, she finally recognized who'd caught her. *Brody.*

He held her in his arms, her body locked against his powerful form, her back to the burning heat of his chest. A low, keening sound of anguish tore through her, and her head dropped forward as hoarse sobs of pain ripped from her throat. "Let me go. I have to help him. *Please,*" she begged brokenly, knowing only that she needed to get to Max. "Let me go, Brody."

He muttered something against her hair, his breath warm against her scalp, and Michaela could have sworn it was a single word…. But she must have heard wrong. She was too upset. Too furious. Too terrified. She must be out of her mind.

Because it sounded as if he'd quietly snarled the word *never.*

Silhouette®

nocturne™

THE FINAL INSTALLMENT OF
THE BLOODRUNNERS TRILOGY

Last Wolf Watching

Runner Brody Carter has found his match in
Michaela Doucet, a human with unusual psychic powers.
When Michaela's brother is threatened, Brody becomes
her protector, and suddenly not only has to protect her
from her enemies but also from himself....

LOOK FOR
LAST WOLF WATCHING
BY
RHYANNON
BYRD

Available May 2008 wherever you buy books.

Dramatic and Sensual Tales of Paranormal Romance

www.eHarlequin.com   SN61786

HARLEQUIN

More Than Words

"The more I see, the more I feel the need."

—**Aviva Presser,** real-life heroine

Aviva Presser is a Harlequin More Than Words
*award winner and the founder of **Bears Without Borders**.*

Discover your inner heroine!

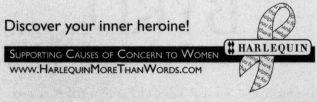

SUPPORTING CAUSES OF CONCERN TO WOMEN ‖ HARLEQUIN

WWW.HARLEQUINMORETHANWORDS.COM

MTW07AP1

HARLEQUIN

More Than Words

"Aviva gives the best bear hugs!"

—**Jennifer Archer,** author

*Jennifer wrote "Hannah's Hugs," inspired by Aviva Presser,
founder of **Bears Without Borders**, a nonprofit organization dedicated
to delivering the comfort and love of a teddy bear to severely ill and
orphaned children worldwide.*

Look for "Hannah's Hugs" in
More Than Words, Vol. 4,
available in April 2008 at eHarlequin.com
or wherever books are sold.

SUPPORTING CAUSES OF CONCERN TO WOMEN ✷ HARLEQUIN
WWW.HARLEQUINMORETHANWORDS.COM

MTW07AP2

REQUEST YOUR FREE BOOKS!

2 FREE NOVELS PLUS 2
FREE GIFTS!

H A R L E Q U I N   R O M A N C E®

From the Heart, For the Heart

YES! Please send me 2 FREE Harlequin Romance® novels and my 2 FREE gifts (gifts are worth about $10). After receiving them, if I don't wish to receive any more books, I can return the shipping statement marked "cancel." If I don't cancel, I will receive 4 brand-new novels every month and be billed just $3.32 per book in the U.S. or $3.80 per book in Canada, plus 25¢ shipping and handling per book and applicable taxes, if any*. That's a savings of over 15% off the cover price! I understand that accepting the 2 free books and gifts places me under no obligation to buy anything. I can always return a shipment and cancel at any time. Even if I never buy another book, the two free books and gifts are mine to keep forever.

114 HDN ERQW   314 HDN ERQ9

Name	(PLEASE PRINT)	
Address		Apt. #
City	State/Prov.	Zip/Postal Code

Signature (if under 18, a parent or guardian must sign)

Mail to the **Harlequin Reader Service:**
IN U.S.A.: P.O. Box 1867, Buffalo, NY 14240-1867
IN CANADA: P.O. Box 609, Fort Erie, Ontario L2A 5X3

Not valid to current subscribers of Harlequin Romance books.

Want to try two free books from another line?
Call 1-800-873-8635 or visit www.morefreebooks.com.

* Terms and prices subject to change without notice. N.Y. residents add applicable sales tax. Canadian residents will be charged applicable provincial taxes and GST. This offer is limited to one order per household. All orders subject to approval. Credit or debit balances in a customer's account(s) may be offset by any other outstanding balance owed by or to the customer. Please allow 4 to 6 weeks for delivery. Offer available while quantities last.

Your Privacy: Harlequin Books is committed to protecting your privacy. Our Privacy Policy is available online at www.eHarlequin.com or upon request from the Reader Service. From time to time we make our lists of customers available to reputable third parties who may have a product or service of interest to you. If you would prefer we not share your name and address, please check here. ☐

HR08

Silhouette

SPECIAL EDITION™

THE WILDER FAMILY
Healing Hearts in Walnut River

Social worker Isobel Suarez was proud to work at Walnut River General Hospital, so when Neil Kane showed up from the attorney general's office to investigate insurance fraud, she was up in arms. Until she melted in his arms, and things got very tricky...

Look for

HER MR. RIGHT?

by

KAREN ROSE SMITH

Available May wherever books are sold.

HARLEQUIN®

American ★ Romance®

Three Boys and a Baby

When Ella Garvey's eight-year-old twins and
their best friend, Dillon, discover an abandoned
baby girl, they fear she will be put in jail—
or worse! They decide to take matters into their
own hands and run away. Luckily the outlaws are
found quickly…and Ella finds a second chance
at love—with Dillon's dad, Jackson.

LOOK FOR

Three Boys and a Baby

BY

LAURA MARIE ALTOM

Available May
wherever you buy books.

LOVE, HOME & HAPPINESS